David Starr Jordan

The Book of Knight and Barbara

Being a Series of Stories Told to Children

David Starr Jordan

The Book of Knight and Barbara
Being a Series of Stories Told to Children

ISBN/EAN: 9783744750462

Printed in Europe, USA, Canada, Australia, Japan

Cover: Foto ©Andreas Hilbeck / pixelio.de

More available books at **www.hansebooks.com**

THE BOOK
OF KNIGHT AND BARBARA

BEING A SERIES OF STORIES
TOLD TO CHILDREN

BY

DAVID STARR JORDAN

*CORRECTED AND ILLUSTRATED
BY THE CHILDREN*

NEW YORK
D. APPLETON AND COMPANY
1899

PREFATORY NOTE.

THE only apology the author can make in this case is that he never meant to do it. He had told his own children many stories of many kinds, some original, some imitative, some travesties of the work of real story-tellers. Two students of the department of Education in the Stanford University—Mrs. Louise Maitland, of San Jose, and Miss Harriet Hawley, of Boston—asked him to repeat these stories before other children. Miss Hawley, as a stenographer, took them down for future reference, and while the author was absent on the Bering Sea Commission of 1896 she wrote them out in full, thus forming the main text of this book. Copies of the stories were placed by Mrs. Maitland in the hands of hundreds of children, most but not all of them in California. These drew illustrative pictures, after their fashion; and from the multitude secured, Mrs. Maitland chose those which are here reproduced.

The scenes in the stories were also subjected to the criticisms of children, and in many cases amended to meet their suggestions. Several of the stories, especially the classical travesties, would not be printed were it not for the children's drawings. These pictures made by the children have been found to interest deeply other children, a fact which gives them a certain value as original documents in the study of the working of the child-mind. At the end of the volume are added a few true stories, mostly of birds and of beasts, told to a different audience. With these are a few drawings by University students, which are intended to assist the imagination of child-readers. "The Story of Bob," and the stories of "Señor Alcatraz," the "Little Blue Fox," and "How the Red Fox went Hunting" are reprinted, by the courtesy of Dr. William Jay Youmans, from Appletons' Popular Science Monthly, and "How the Commander Sailed," from the Pacific Monthly, by the courtesy of Mr. W. Bittle Wells. The indebtedness of the author to Mrs. Maitland and to Miss Hawley is indicated above.

DAVID STARR JORDAN.

PALO ALTO, CAL., *August 10, 1899.*

CONTENTS.

THE BOOK OF KNIGHT AND BARBARA.

HOW BARBARA CAME TO ESCONDITÉ.

ONCE there was a little girl and she lived all alone in a little house up in the woods on a mountain, and the little house wasn't any big-

The place where she lived.

ger than this room, but it had in it a kitchen where she did her cooking, and a little dining-room where she ate her dinner, and a little bedroom where she slept. The little bedroom had in it a little bed for the little girl and tiny beds for her dolls. And there were tables, dishes, pictures on the walls, and little electric lights to light up her room with when it was night with electricity that came from the lightning.

The little girl had three little dolls, and one little doll's name was Marguerite, and she had red

. Dancing fairies on the green.

hair and lots of it, and it was real hair too. Another little doll's name was Sally, and she had black hair—not real hair, but just painted on—and her head was made of porcelain, like dishes. The other little doll which was a boy doll, and a Chinaman at that, hadn't any hair at all, and so he was called Old Baldy.

He finds the house.

Lots of fairies lived near this little girl on the mountain, and they used to come and visit her and sit by the table with her. They liked the little girl, and so they made her queen of the fairies. And out around in the woods on the mountain there were many coyotes. They troubled the fairies very much and chased them in the night when they were dancing on the green, and then all the little fairies would scamper off to their holes, and they were lucky if some of them did not get caught by the old coyote.

One night the little girl was sleeping in her little bed in the little bedroom, with a doll on each side of her and Old Baldy across the foot of the bed, when

The coyote breaks into the room.

she heard a big coyote come up on the front steps. The coyote looked into the window and howled, "Willie wau woo! willie wau woo! wito hooh!" Then he howled again and pushed the window right in and came in to where the little girl was. The little girl grabbed her dolls, so that the coyote would not get them. Then she took the little red-haired doll Marguerite, and when the coyote opened his mouth wide she pushed the dolly right down his throat. The red hair tickled him and made him

The red-headed doll is in his throat.

sneeze, and he sneezed and sneezed until he sneezed his old head off. Then the little girl was glad, and she got up and took the coyote by the hind leg and

She drags the coyote under the tree.

dragged him out under the tree. Then she picked up his old head and carried that off too. Then she

went back and washed the coyote-stuff all off from
the floor. When that was done she put her dollies
to bed, and then she went to sleep again herself.

She wipes up the coyote-stuff.

When the other coyotes came around in the night
and saw what she had done they were very much
afraid.

In the morning when the fairies found it out
they were very glad, and they rubbed fairy-stuff on
the doll Marguerite and made her alive again. Then
they all had such a good time—the little girl and
the fairies and the dolls. They cooked and ate and
played in the grass, and the coyotes all ran away

from the mountain and didn't trouble them any more.

One day I was walking in the woods on the mountain and I saw the little girl asleep on the grass. So I woke her up and took her on my back and walked way down the mountain with her and along the road clear to Escondité, where we used to live. When the little girl got to Escondité she

When he took her home.

looked at the trees and the roses and the monkeys in the barn, and she said she would stay there. And she has lived at our house ever since. When the fairies came around her little house in the woods they saw that the little girl was gone, and at first

2

they felt badly, but when they found the little red-
haired doll named Marguerite they made her their
queen and fixed up the little house very nicely for
her and for Old Baldy, and she has been queen of the
fairies ever since; and if you look up on the mountain on a dark night you will see the little electric
lights that shine all night from her bedroom window
so that the fairies can see to dance on the grass.

THERE once was a Baron Munchausen,
    He surely was one of a thousan',
        For the stories he told
        They can never grow old,
So long as the small boy is browsin'.

THE LITTLE LEGS THAT RAN AWAY.

ONCE there was a little girl and she used to take off her little legs when she went to bed at night and put them with her clothes and the rest of her things in a chair. And one night the little legs got uneasy and ran away. They found the

Took off her little legs when she went to bed.

bedroom door open, so they ran down the steps into the garden and across the gravel walk out into the fields, and away so far no one could see them. When the little girl woke up in the morning she

found that her legs were gone, so she couldn't
walk. And so she began to cry until her mother
came in, and then they looked all around for the little legs. When they went out into the garden they
saw the prints on the gravel which the little legs had
made on going out, for it had just been raining and
you could see the marks quite plainly. So her
father saddled the horses, and they got on their
backs and cantered around all over the fields and
down the road and looked for the little legs. By
and by they saw something running by the side of

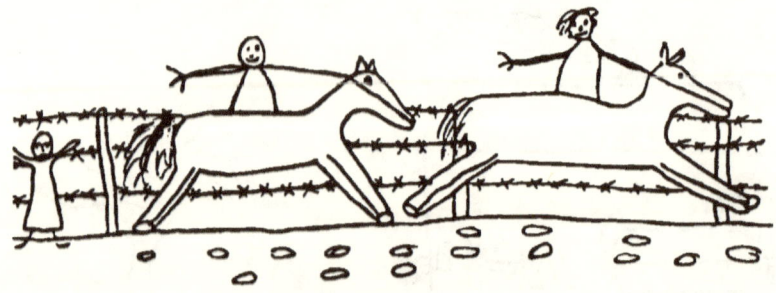

They saw the prints on the gravel.

the road away down toward the Bay. Then they
whipped up the horses, and they ran very fast, and
the father got off from his horse and caught the
little legs just as they were getting tangled in a
barbed wire fence. Then he picked up the little
legs and wrapped them in a soft blanket and put

them under his coat and carried them home. Then they fastened them on again, so that the little girl could make them carry her around anywhere she wanted to go; and ever since then she has kept them stuck on tight, so they can't get away, and she never, never takes them off at night.

Tangled in a barbed wire fence.

A little boy, and he had a wooden sword.

THE BOY THAT WHACKED THE WITCH'S TOADSTOOLS.

ONCE there was a little boy and he had a wooden sword, and he went out into the woods whacking the thistles. One day he saw a great lot of white toadstools, and so he went for them and knocked them

The little boy knocked down the toadstools.

all down with his wooden sword. When the old witch that had made them all for the goblins to sit on, came along and saw what he had been doing, she felt very bad, and cried for half an hour. Then she rode back to the place where she lived and got

some witch-stuff she had made out of the teeth of
black cats soaked in formalin, and that night when
the little boy was fast asleep she got on a broom-

The old witch came along.

stick and rode to his house, and came down the
chimney into his room, and rubbed witch-stuff all
over him. The little boy was fast asleep and knew

She rode back to the place where she lived.

nothing about it, but in the morning when his
mother came into his room to see why he didn't get
up, she could not find him anywhere. All at once

he jumped up from under the bed, and his mother
saw that he was all covered over with hair, for he
was turned into a little monkey person, and he chattered and chattered, and showed his teeth as he
jumped around. So his mother got a belt and put
it around his waist, and tied a rope to the belt, and
fastened him to the bed. He sat on the foot of the
bed all day, and at night he went to sleep, and his

He was a little monkey person.

mother tucked him up in his little bed, with his
monkey face against 'the white pillows, and she
hoped that something would happen to make him
better before morning.

In the morning when his mother came in she
heard a strange sound in the room, as though some one
called out, "Knee-deep! knee-deep! you'll drown!
you'll drown!" and she saw that the monkey was

gone, and in his place there was a great green frog.
And the frog jumped around on the floor, and into
the washbowl, and into the pitcher. When he got
into the pitcher he couldn't jump out, so he stayed
there all day. At night he went to sleep. Then

She took him out of the water pitcher.

his mother came into the room, and took him out
of the water pitcher and put him into bed, and
straightened out his little green legs under the
blankets. Then she went away.

In the morning she came around to the room and
again heard somebody going, "Hoo, hoo, hoo!" She
said she'd like to know "who." So she went in to
find out. The frog was gone; but instead of the
little boy there was a little bird with a long hooked
bill like a parrot, all covered over with feathers. It
was a little owl, and it called out "Hoo, hoo, hoo!" all

the time. His mother could hardly hold him in her arms, he had such sharp claws and such a hooked bill. He went to sleep when she was holding him, and then she put him to bed, where he lay all day, for an owl sleeps all day long. But at night she could hardly get him to sleep. She took him in her arms and rocked him and rocked him; then she laid him

It was a little owl.

down in the bed, straightened out his little legs with the crooked toes, and turned up his little hooked nose, and then she went away.

The next morning early she heard somebody in the room, going "Oo-eu-oo-a-oo." She went in there, and sure enough, instead of the little boy there was a big rooster sitting on the head of the bed, crowing away with all his might. His mother said she had had enough of that, so she stuck some pins into him and he stopped crowing, and wherever one of

those pins stuck a pinfeather grew out. Then she
took hold of the rooster and pulled all his feathers

Crowing away with all his might.

out. When she had pulled out every one he didn't
feel quite so smart as he did before, and then he was
willing to go to bed early. So his mother tucked
him up into bed, and straightened out his claws, and
tied a handkerchief around his bare neck.

A little speckly, jumpy pig.

In the morning she came in again. "Ugh, ugh!"
she heard, and there was a little speckly, jumpy pig

in the bed.   His mother said that this was just a little too much for her, so took the pig by one of his hind legs and put him in the bathtub.   Then she rubbed him and she scrubbed him with sapolio and benzine, and he squealed and squealed; but his

mother kept at it until she had rubbed all the witch-stuff off, and then the pig part all came off. Then she rubbed him all over with vaseline until he became a little boy again, just the same as he was before.

And ever since then when he has had a wooden sword he has worn it by his side, and kept away from toadstools.   And when the witch saw him once more, she wanted to know how he got to be a boy again, and he wouldn't tell her.

A Union soldier now.

But when she wanted some one to come and be a king she sent for this little boy.

THE KING WHOSE EYES WERE OPENED.

ONCE there was a witch and she sat by the side of the road, and she was crying, for she felt very badly because the little boy had broken down her toadstools. The king came driving by, and the witch came up to him and asked the king to give her something; but the king shut his eyes and wouldn't look at her. Then the witch began to cry louder than ever, and the king shut his eyes all the tighter, and drove on. Then said the witch: "When you get ready to open your eyes, I will see that they stay open."

When the king got ready to open his eyes he opened them very wide, because he saw such astonishing things. He looked up into the sky, and all of a sudden he saw the dragon of the great Pendragon ship going by in the clouds—sailing away through the sky all full of dragons. Dragons on one hand and dragons on the other, dragons on the sails and dragons on the masts—green dragons, blue drag-

ons, yellow dragons. The king opened his eyes still
wider when he saw all this, and when he opened
them wide enough he could see everything on earth,
and everything that was going on everywhere. So
he kept opening his eyes wider and wider, because

The king came driving by.

there were so many things he didn't know before.
He looked up into the sky and he could see the
moon and everything there was on it, the man in
the moon and all the things he had—calves and
chickens and pigs and briar bushes. He looked into
the sun—the sun was wide open, and he could see

into the middle of it and all the things that were there.

When he got to the palace his eyes were open so wide, looking at all these things, that he stepped right out through his eyelids, and then he was in all sorts of trouble. He couldn't walk any more nor do anything, and so they had to carry him up and put him on his throne. When he sat on the throne he could see all sorts of wonderful things he had never heard of before, for he was looking right down into himself.

Then they sent for the witch to come and help the king. "Your eyes are open a good deal wider than you wanted," the witch said. " Trade places with me ; go out on the road and look at things, and let me be queen for ten years. Then I will put some witch-stuff on your eyes that will make them all right again, so that you can shut your eyes, and then you can not see half as much as you do now." And the king said he would be glad to trade places. Then the witch went into the palace and was queen, and the king went out on the road. But he still had some of the witch-stuff on his eyes, and his eyes were open a little wider   other people's eyes. He walked along the roa·   fter day, and saw all

the little crickets that live under a stone, saw how
all the little flowers open their buds, and saw the
little birds build their nests in the trees, and saw the

He walked along the road day after day.

little fishes gathering their broods in the brooks.
He liked going along the road looking at things so
much that, when the ten years were up, he did not
want to be king any more at all. Then he went off
where the witch couldn't find him. But the witch
was tired of being queen, for she wanted to get out
and plant some new toadstools. So when the ten
years were passed and she couldn't find the king she
went away, and there was no king nor queen. But
the witch found the little boy that had whacked her

toadstools, and she got him to be king, and he is king yet, and sits on a great golden throne, with a wooden sword in his hand and a golden crown on his head. And if you will look into the window of the back parlor of the palace you will see him sitting there to-day.

And he is king yet.

ONCE there was a little boy and his name was Candytuft, and his little sister was named Daffodil. So their father and mother went away one day and left them all alone at home; and when it came time for supper all they could find in the pantry were two crackers, and one of these was a firecracker. So the little boy, whose name was Candytuft, looked around in all the grates till he found a spark of fire. Then he put the end of the firecracker on the·spark of fire, and it went fizz-ziz-bang! and the little boy jumped and the little girl screamed.

For there stood a great, big, black genius, with hair like a broom and whiskers like a mop, and great rolling eyes. Then the genius bowed low and said, "What does my Lord Candytuft want?" And the little boy was astonished, but he thought it a good chance to get some more firecrackers. So he said that he wanted a hundred bunches of firecrackers, and a magic match to light them with, and a genius

24

to come for every one. So the genius scratched a
match on his heel, and a dwarf came, with a red cap
and yellow gloves, and brought the firecrackers and
the match. But the genius said that the little boy
must not be piggish;
there were not genii
enough to go around,
and one big genius
would have to do for
the whole hundred
bunches of firecrackers.

Then the genius
vanished away, but the
little boy had him back
again very soon, and
then the little girl said
that it was her turn.

The dwarf came, with red cap and
yellow gloves.

So she burned a firecracker, and the genius came
back and bowed very low, saying: "What does my
Lady Daffodil want?". "I want a hundred dolls,"
said the little girl. So the dwarf brought in a
hundred dolls and stood them up around the wall.
Then the dwarf and the genius vanished away. But
the little boy took his magic match and lighted a
firecracker. And it went fizz-ziz-bang! just as be-

fore, and the genius had to come back to see what the little boy wanted. And he had to come so often after that, that he finally went out to the barn and made a bed in the hay instead of vanishing away in the regular fashion of genii. And he took the dwarf with him and made him a nice little bed of cotton batting in an old cracker box; but this was just a box for common crackers, not firecrackers.

So when the little boy or the little girl looked toward the barn and called out, the genius came and the dwarf with them, and they didn't have to burn any more firecrackers.

Then the little girl wanted her dolls dressed, and the dwarf dressed them all. And the little boy called for tin soldiers—and they wanted them to talk and to walk. So the dwarf rubbed fairy-stuff on all the tin soldiers and on all the dolls, so that they could all talk and walk, and they had great fun. And the tin soldiers danced with the dolls, and the genius got a fine supper, and the dwarf waited at the table. Then they had a nice dance and a lot of pretty little games, such as " Sing a Song of Sixpence " and " Ring around the Rosy," that the little boy and the little girl had learned at the kindergarten.

And in the evening, after the dwarf had put all

the dolls to bed in a lot of little beds the genius had made, the tin soldiers spread their blankets on the floor and they all slept until morning.

Then, next day, they all went out for a walk in the woods. They went out by the brook, taking good care to keep out of the way of the poison oak, till they came to the open place behind the thick forest. Here they all sat down for a lunch, and then they took a nap, and the little boy slept in the genius's cap, and the little girl in one of his shoes, while the dwarf curled up in another.

But when they were fast asleep a fox came along and grabbed one of the little dolls and a coyote took another. The dolls screamed while they were being swallowed, but it was no use. Down they went.

Then the genius sent the dwarf out, and he caught the fox by his bushy tail and made him unswallow the little doll. And he rubbed fairy-stuff on the doll so that she came to be all right again, and he rubbed fairy-stuff on the fox and he became tame and all good-natured like the rest of them. And he did the same with the coyote, and when they came home the little boy rode on the coyote's back and the little girl on the fox's back, and the genius

went ahead and the dwarf behind, and every little
doll rode home on the back of a tin soldier.

And when they came home they all sat down together on the front steps, except the genius, who was
so big that he sat all over the yard, when their folks
came driving up the road on their way home. And
when their mother saw the genius and the fox and
the coyote and everything else she was very much
scared. And the genius got up very quickly and
stepped on the magic match, setting all the firecrackers on fire. And they all went fizz-ziz-bang so
fast that the genius couldn't keep time with them,
for he had to jump up at every firecracker and bow
and ask what my lord wanted. And jumping
around in that way he was scared out of his wits
and ran away, and the dwarf ran too, and the tin
soldiers and the dolls, and nobody has seen any of
them since. Only there were three little dolls that
didn't have any fairy-stuff rubbed on them, and they
stayed in the corner all alone and didn't run away.
And one of these was named Marguerite, and she
had long red hair. And one was Sally, and she had
black hair just painted on, and the other was a little
Chinese doll with no hair at all, and they called him
Old Baldy. And there was one tin soldier that was

broken in two because the genius had stepped on him, and so he was left behind. He was not of any use until they fastened him together with glue, and then he was all right again.

The little boy felt very badly until his father got him a hundred more bunches of firecrackers. Then he fired them all off, but the old genius did not come back any more, nor any other genius.

I think that the reason was because he had lost the magic match. But it may be because the genius was busy with some other little boy over in Crim Tartary, where all the genii live. Maybe some Fourth of July, or some Chinese New Year's, when he hasn't so much to do, the genius will come back again, and then the little boy will take good care that his mother does not scream when she sees him, and so scare him off.

THE MAGIC THIMBLE.

ONCE there was a little girl and she had a name
so pretty that I could never say it, and nobody
could ever print it in a book, so I will call her Rainbow, but that was not her real name. When her
birthday came, Santa Claus brought her a little thimble, not a common one, but a magic thimble, such as
the magic people have. Santa Claus had just come
back from Crim Tartary, where all the children have
magic toys, and all toys are alive, and griffins and
genii are just as common as canary birds and kittens
are with us. So he got the magic thimble mixed up
with the other things, and the little girl found it in
her stocking along with the rest of her toys.

And when she put it on to mend her little stocking, she pricked it with her needle, and there came a
snap and a spark of fire, something went buzz-buzz,
and a little girl genius stood before her, and said:
" What does Rainbow want ? " And Rainbow looked
at the little girl genius, and saw her pink dress and
30

blue sash and round blue eyes. And she said: "I want a little doll, just like you." And then the little genius went out through the keyhole, and the little girl looked in her doll's house, and sure enough there was a nice little doll just like the genius, with pink dress and blue sash, and she sat there and stared with her blue eyes wide open at the little girl. So the little girl played with her doll, and she named it Leila, and she had such a nice time; but the little doll couldn't do anything—only sit and stare.

So the little girl pricked her thimble again and it went snap, buzz-buzz, and the little girl genius came back again, and she said: "What does Rainbow want?" And she wanted her little doll to see out of her eyes. So the genius went out of the window, and the doll Leila could see out of her eyes, so she didn't have to stare any more; but that was all she could do.

And when the little girl called up the genius again she wanted her doll to talk. And so it was. The doll talked and talked all the time, but she didn't say anything. She talked of her dresses, how many she had and how many more she wanted, and one was pink and her sash was blue, and she said this all over so many times that the little girl said she was silly, and she didn't like her at all, and then she cried and cried till Rainbow tied a ribbon over her mouth to keep her still. Then she got out the magic thimble once more. And then the little girl wished that Leila would talk some sense. Then she did talk sense, for the little girl genius made it so. Then the little girl talked with the doll all day, and talked good sense, and she has done so ever since, and it is ever so nice.

But she had to carry Leila everywhere in her arms. So she got the thimble and called the little girl genius up again. The genius didn't like it very well, because she was in a hurry, and wanted to get back to Crim Tartary, where all the rest of the genii live, and she knew that her father and mother would miss her.

But the little girl kept her busy all the time, for now she wanted the doll Leila to walk. And the doll walked all about, but she was so small that she got lost in the flower garden, and gave the little girl lots of trouble. So the next time Rainbow put on her thimble she wished that Leila would grow bigger every day, just as she did, and then she wouldn't keep getting lost all the time. But the little girl genius smiled and said it would be easier to bring her a little sister and be done with it, instead of fixing up the doll Leila any more.

So the little girl genius brought Rainbow a little sister, and she had a name just as pretty as Rainbow's, so pretty that I can't say it at all, and it could never be printed in any book. And Rainbow played with her little sister every day, and forgot all about the magic thimble, and all about the doll Leila. And the doll Leila put the thimble on her little hand, and all her fingers went into it, and then she pricked the thimble with a pin, and the little girl genius came up, and then they both went off together and took the thimble with them. And the little girl never saw them any more, and I never did either, but I think that they must have gone back to Crim Tartary, where all the dolls can talk and all the children's playthings are magic.

UNA'S CHILDREN AND THE LION.

(As Dictated and Illustrated by Barbara.)

ONCE there was a little girl and Una was the mother, you know (for Una had a lion that used to walk with her in the woods). And Una said that she could have the lion, and Una told the children

Una, with stirrups, on the lion.

that they could have the lion if they could hitch him up well. And then Una had the lion after the

34

Una's father and mother.

Una's children ride on the lion.

children had him, and then the lion went with the children whenever they wanted him to.   And the lion loved the children and Una.

And oh, the children rode him every day, and all the time when Una wasn't using him.   They had a little saddle of course, a sidesaddle.

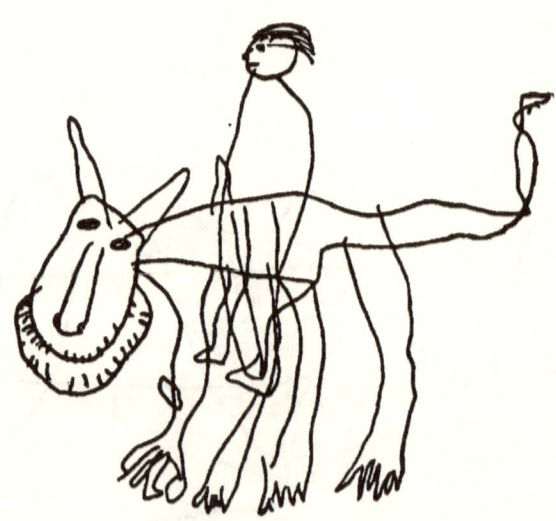

Una's father rides the lion.

THE BOY AND GIRL WHO SAILED AWAY.

ONCE there were two children, a little boy and a little girl, and they lived by the side of a lake. In the lake there was a boat, and they got into the boat, and then the boy spread the sail, and the little

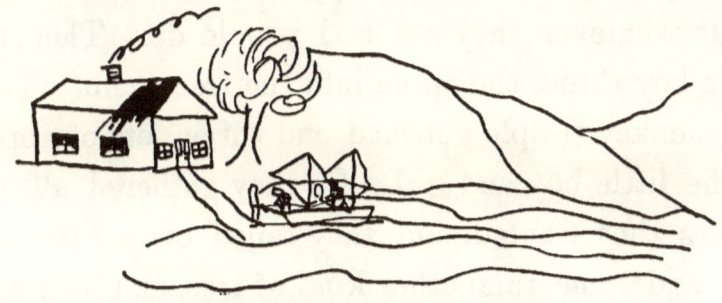

They lived by the side of a lake.

girl took hold of the rudder, and the little boy took the hatchet that he found in the boat and chopped off the rope, and the boat sailed away, out of sight of home, off into strange countries, and down a strange river. It sailed along until it was night, and then it sailed until it came morning. The children were very hungry in the morning, and they sailed under a big tree full of monkey people. It was a wild apple tree, and monkeys were on all its branches. They hadn't anything left in their boat to eat except one graham gem, and they took this one gem and threw it at the monkey people, and the monkey people threw an apple back, for they have to do whatever they see real people do. Then the little boy threw the apple into the tree again. Then the monkey people got mad, and threw lots of apples at the little boy and girl. So they gathered all the apples they wanted, and they sailed on a little farther and came to another kind of tree, and it was a breadfruit tree, and that was full of monkey people too. So the little boy and girl threw apples at the monkey people, and the monkey persons threw down breadfruit at them. So then after they had gathered all the breadfruit they wanted they sailed on again.

But they had nothing to eat on their bread. They came next to a hollow tree, and this tree had a squirrel in it, and he had lots of nuts stored away inside. They took all the nuts he had, and the squirrel said he might as well go along too. Then they came to a bee tree, and the squirrel went out and made a hole in the bee tree. Then the little

boy took some matches he found in the bottom of
the boat, and lighted them, and put them into the
hole in the bee tree, and the burning matches made
the bees all go to sleep, and the little boy reached in

The monkey persons threw breadfruit at them.

and got all the honey they wanted. Then they cut
their bread into slices and put honey on it and ate
it. But at home they always used to toast their
bread, so they found a bottle and filled it with
water and held it in the sun; in that way they made
a burning glass, and they toasted their bread by it.

4

They went on a little farther, and the first thing they knew the squirrel had been gnawing away in the bottom of the boat, and had cut a hole in it, so that the water came in and the boat began to sink. The little boy waded out into the water, and the bottom was covered with clam shells. Then he saw a big India-rubber tree growing on the bank. So he took one of the clam shells and fastened it on the India-rubber tree, and cut a hole in the tree with his jackknife. Then lots of India-rubber milk ran out of the tree and he caught it in the clam shell. Then he took the milk and filled up the hole in the boat with it. Then they made a cover of India rubber to go over the boat when it was raining, and they made some rubber boots, rubber bands, and rubber ropes, to use when they needed them. It was very lucky that they did so, for pretty soon a great storm came up, and the water went all over the boat, and carried away the masts and sails. When the storm was over they saw it was not a storm at all, but a great big whale had been spouting and had done it all. When the little boy saw the whale he took his hatchet and cut a whalebone out of its mouth, and put it up for a mast. Then all around them they saw a flock of Portuguese men-of-war. They caught

They caught the Portuguese men-of-war.

a lot of these and fastened them together and made new sails of them. They made very nice sails, for they are soft as silk, and blue and pink, and all sorts of colors.

By and by a big snake poked his head out at them from a hole in the bank, as if he were going to bite somebody. But the little boy was ready for everything. He took a rubber band and clapped it around the snake's mouth. Then he fastened the snake's tail to a tree and held on to its head; and so they used the snake for an anchor. Then a pelican came along and they asked him if he would like to ride with them. He said he would, so the little boy put a rubber band around his neck and a rubber strap around his leg. Then the pelican went fishing, but he could not swallow the fishes he caught because there was a band around his neck. When he had caught a fish they pulled him in by the strap on his leg, and so they got all the fishes they wanted.

But their parents at home were very much worried, because they did not know where the children were. Finally they got a steamboat and started out to find them. They came along to the monkey people, who threw apples at them. Then they came to the breadfruit tree, and the monkeys there threw breadfruit at them so that they didn't dare to stay on the outside of the boat. But they didn't know that breadfruit was good to eat. Then they came to the bee tree. The bees had all waked up by that time; so they flew out and stung them. They sailed away in a hurry, for their faces smarted where they had been stung. Then they came to where the India-rubber tree was. They thought that it would make their faces feel better, if they rubbed India-rubber milk over the sore places. But the rubber stuck tight to their faces. They drank some of the India-rubber milk, and it turned hard, and then they couldn't get their mouths open, and when they finally opened their mouths the rubber pulled all their teeth out.

So they sailed on to where the children were. The old snake that had been the anchor stuck out his tail, and it went into their boat and scared them; then it got tangled up in the wheel of the steamer, and splashed the water all over the old folks. When the children saw their parents coming, they were very nice to them. They called to them not to be afraid, for they would take care of them. Then they went over to the steamboat and took the old folks into their own boat, and they gave them

some breadfruit and toast
and honey, and nice things,
and treated them as well as
they could, and went home,
and carried the old folks safely home with them. They
fastened the snake's tail to
the bowsprit, and dragged
the steamboat home behind
them.

GOBLINS live in Goblintown—
    Funniest place I know;
Half the houses upside down,
    Goblins build 'em so.

Some with doorsteps in the air,
    Chimneys underground;
Goblins make them anyhow,
    Leave them standing round.

Just the way the goblins have,
    Nothing fixed up right;
Goblins lie and sleep all day,
    Have to work at night.

All the streets in Goblintown
    Don't run anywhere;
Seem to go just round and round;
    Goblins do not care.

Lots of fun in Goblintown,
   Circus every night;
Can't make goblins go to school
   Just to read and write.

Goblins queerest kind of folks,
   Look like great big flies;
Have balloons instead of heads,
   Bottle glass for eyes.

Goblins pull their heads right off,
   Toss them in the sky;
When you think they're gone for good,
   Catch them on the fly.

Goblins whittle toadstools out
   While they're standing round;
When there's nothing else to do,
   Stick 'em in the ground.

When a goblin wants to fly
   All he has to do,
Just to flap his ears and howl,
   Then away he'll go.

Want to go to Goblintown?
   Only just one way;

Just you take some pitch-dark night
   When the moon's away.

Don't you say a single word,
   Just you go to bed;
Let your mamma tuck you in,
   Little sleepy head.

Just pretend to go to sleep,
   As you always do,
Till you hear the old town clock
   Striking one or two.

Then you just crawl out of bed,
   Creep right down the stair,
Go and stand behind the pump—
   Always goblins there.

Call out, " Goblin, goblin, come ! "
   And they'll run to you;
Then they'll beat the goblin drum,
   As they always do.

Climb upon the goblin's back,
   Hold on tight, of course;
Canter off to Goblintown
   On a goblin horse.

Lose your way in Goblintown?
    Awful easy to;
First you know you're somewhere else,
    Someone else is you.

Get you home from Goblintown?
    Guess you'd better stay
Till you hear the breakfast bell;
    That's the quickest way.

The turkey-buzzard.

THE STRANGE RABBIT.

ONCE there was a turkey - buzzard, and he flew over the country flapping his wings. One day he saw sitting on the rock in the sun what he thought was a big fat rabbit, so says he, "Let's have that rabbit for dinner." But the rabbit said nothing. Then the turkey - buzzard flew down and grabbed the rab-

Went like a buzz saw.

What he really saw.

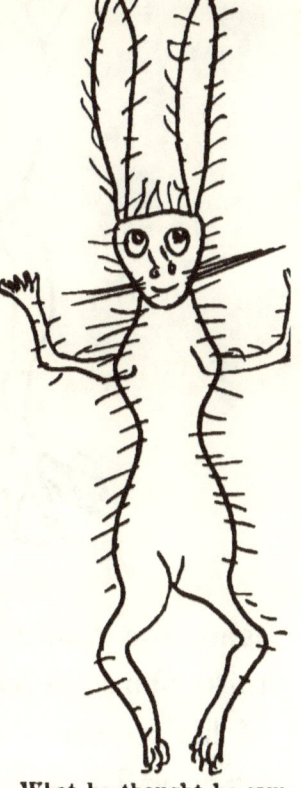

What he thought he saw.

49

bit and the rabbit went, "r-r-r wu-wu-wu," just like
a buzz saw, and the turkey-buzzard found himself
rolling all over the ground, and when it was all quiet

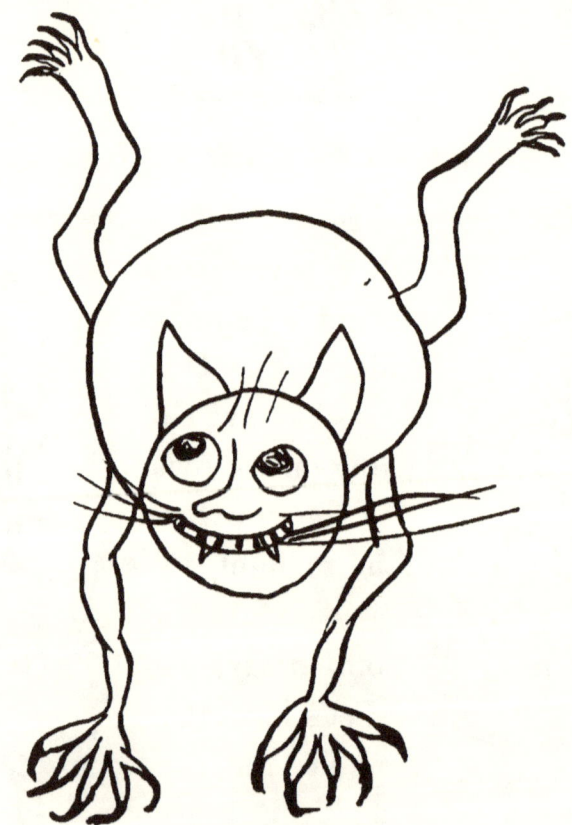

It turned around.

again the rabbit wasn't saying anything. But the
turkey-buzzard looked around and could not find any
of his feathers, for they were lying all about in the
grass, and one half his bill was gone, and he had

only one leg. These pictures show what the turkey-buzzard thought he saw, and what he really saw, and what it looked like when it turned around, and the way the turkey-buzzard looked when he was walking home.

When he walked home.

THE KING THAT HAD NO CASTLE.

ONCE there wasn't any king and he did not have any castle, and his castle wasn't made out of stone, and it wasn't just set down on the ground, so that whoever came in and out its big iron door did not have to walk in the dust. And so the king wasn't unhappy, because the dust did not get on his clothes in dry weather, and he wasn't spattered with mud when it rained. For that is just the way it is with common folks who are not kings and who haven't any castles, and so can not come indoors when it is wet.

So the king didn't get tired of his castle, because it wasn't just set on the ground. So he didn't go out in the evening and sit on the doorstep, looking up into the clouds, which were not piling up on each other like great mountains, and he didn't wish that he had built his castle up there where he would never get dust on his clothes, nor bespatter his shoes with mud. And so when he had not looked at the

52

clouds for a long time, he did not order his horse
and his soldiers and ride up the side of the mountain, high up to where the pinnacles of stone do not
rise above the rolling cliffs of the cloud. So he did
not take his soldiers and his horse and ride out on
the great clouds, which were not piled up black
before him, with red edges where the light of the
setting sun did not shine slantwise across them.

Then he did not pitch his tent on the clouds for
the night, and sleep quietly where there wasn't any
noise at all. For up in the clouds there were not
any trees for the wind to rustle through. And there
wasn't any dust in the air and the dirt was not
thickened into mud, because there wasn't any ground
at all, only air and clouds.

So when it wasn't night any more, the king
did not wake up to look at the sunrise. And
the bright sun did not shine on the clouds and did
not melt them. And so the king and his soldiers
did not fall out of their cloud castle into the loose
naked air, because there weren't any castles, and
the king and his soldiers were not any of them
there.

But if they had been there it would have been
bad for the king, don't you think so? And after he

had slept in the cloud castle one night, he would have been glad to get back to his stone castle on earth, and to the dirt on which all the kings there are, and all the other folks, must build whatever kind of castles they have.

THE SIX KINGS OF YVETÔT.

THERE were six kings of Yvetôt,
　　They stood up in an awful row,
And every time they looked around
They cast their eyes upon the ground,
And when they saw their eyes were gone,
They, just the same, kept staring on ;
Then threw their arms up in the air
Until they had no arms to spare.
But if a queen or two came near,
Then every king would lend an ear ;
And if the queen had cheeks of red,
Then every king would lose his head.

I do not like to look at kings,
They do such very awful things ;
And actions such as these must tend
To make one's hair stand up on end.

5

THE GHOST WITH THE HORSEHAIR WIG.

ONCE there was an old church and it stood by the river, and nobody went to meeting there, and so it got full of owls and ghosts. And the owls sat up in the tower and asked "Who? Who? Who?" all the time. They never waited for any answer, and they have never yet found out Who. The seats had all been taken out of the church to fit up the new church over in the town, so the ghosts went into the empty space where the seats had been.

The ghosts used to dance in the church every night and they had lots of fun, because they could just dance right through each other, and they could dance on the ceiling just as well as on the floor, and they could dance all night without getting warm or tired, because they hadn't any bones in them or any blood—just a lot of ghost-stuff held together by some white clothes. And they could see in the dark just as well as in the daytime, because their eyes shone like electric lights.

And when they were having a great time dancing and singing ghost songs that nobody but ghosts can hear, there came a man riding by on a bay mare, and he rode up close and looked into the window.

They were having great fun, and one ghost that could jump higher than any of the others skipped around so that the man outside shouted, " Well done! Do it again ! "

And all the ghosts heard him and they were very mad. And they came out of the church like a swarm of bees and ran after the man. When he saw them coming he whipped the bay mare, and she ran as fast as she could toward the bridge over the river. Now ghosts are made so that when they come to a running stream they can't get across it, but just go off into mist. With goblins it is different; the only thing goblins are afraid of is fire, and they can paddle in the water just like ducks.

So the ghosts leaped after him, and the horse ran till she came right up on the bridge. But the ghost that could jump the highest ran ahead of the rest and got the old mare by the tail, and off the tail came. So the man rode home in the dark on the old bay mare which had not any tail. And the

ghost wears the horse's tail for hair; and if you ever
go by the old church by the bridge of Doon at mid-
night, and look into the window, you will see that
the ghost that can jump the highest is the one that
wears a black horsehair wig.

THE MOUSE'S DREAM.

ONCE there was a mouse and he got into the
cupboard and ate all the cheese he could hold,
and when he went back to bed in his little nest in
the hay-mow he dreamed that he had swallowed a
cat, and when he woke up in the morning this is all
that he could remember of his dream.

All he could remember of his dream.

IVEDE-AVEDE AND THE DRAGONS.

ONCE there was a king, and his daughter was stolen away by a dragon, and the dragon carried her down into a deep well, and dropped her into the water, and then sat on the rocks over her head to

The dragon.

see that she stayed there. So I don't know what the king would have done if it hadn't been for a boy who lived near by, whose name was Ivede-Avede. This little boy saw the dragon and the princess there, so he jumped down into the well, and when he came down he broke the dragon's neck. Then he was down there alone with the princess, and the cold water was up to their shoulders, and made them both shiver.

Stolen away by a dragon.

By and by the mate of the dragon came along
and flew down backward into the well, just as
dragons do, not suspecting that anything was wrong.
Then the little boy, Ivede-Avede, took hold of the
princess with one hand and with the other he took
the dragon whose neck was broken, and pinched its
mouth tight on to the other dragon's tail.   The live

He jumped down into the well.

dragon was very much scared and flew out, screaming with all his might, for he did not know what
was biting him.   But Ivede-Avede held tight to the
dead dragon's head, holding the teeth fast on the
live dragon's tail.   And he kept the princess on his
other arm, and so they were both hauled out to the
top of the well.   Then he let go, and the dragon

He pinched its mouth on to the other dragon's tail.

sailed off high into the air with the dead dragon fast
on his tail.

Then the little boy
took the princess home
to his house and put dry
things on, and the prin-
cess put on some of his
mother's old clothes — a
red petticoat and an old
yellow sunbonnet. Then
when they were all warm
and dry he hitched his
horse, Old Charley, to his
father's buckboard and
started off across the mountain to the king's palace

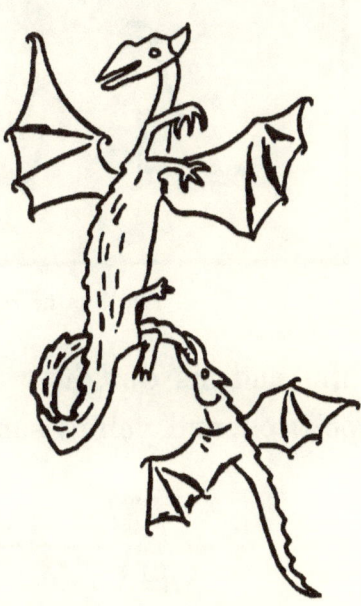

With the dead dragon fast on
his tail.

with the princess. When he came driving across the
garden of the palace, the king was very glad to see

On the way to the palace.

Told him he might marry the princess.

him and his daughter safe and sound, with the red
petticoat and yellow sunbonnet. So the king took off

They had a great wedding.

his crown and bowed, and thanked Ivede-Avede, and
invited him to stay to dinner, and told him that if
he liked he might marry the princess. Ivede-Avede
said that he had to take Old Charley back home first,
and when he had done that he would come to dinner
at the king's palace. And so he drove the horse back

The princess painting dragons on the plates.

to his father's house, and then put on his Sunday
clothes and walked over the mountain to the palace.
The king and the princess met him at the garden
gate, and they had a great wedding, and there was a
picture of a dragon on each one of the plates at the
table. The princess had painted them all while
Ivede-Avede was taking Old Charley back to his

father's house. But he forgot to take home the red petticoat and the yellow sunbonnet, and if you ever go to the king's palace you can see them, for the princess has them yet.

There was a picture of a dragon on each plate.

THE OGRE THAT PLAYED JACKSTRAWS.

ONCE there was a terrible giant ogre, and he lived in a huge castle that was built right in the middle of a valley. All men had to pass by it when they came to the king's palace on the rock at the head of the valley. And they were all terribly afraid of the ogre, and ran just as fast as they could when they went by. And when they looked back as they were running, they could see the ogre sitting on the wall of his castle. And he scowled at them so fiercely that they ran as fast as ever they could. For the ogre had a head as large as a barrel, and great black eyes sunk deep under long bushy eyelashes. And when he opened his mouth they saw that it was full of teeth, and so. they ran away faster than ever, without caring to see anything more.

And the king wanted to get rid of the ogre, and he sent his men to drive the ogre away and to tear down his castle. But the ogre scowled at them so

67

savagely that their teeth began to fall out, and they
all turned back and said they dare not fight such a
horrid creature.   Then Roger, the king's son, rode
his black horse Hurricane up against the door of

Roger and his horse Hurricane.

the ogre's castle, and struck hard against the door
with his iron glove.   Then the door opened and the
ogre came out and seized Roger in one hand and the
great black horse in the other and rubbed their
heads together, and while he did this he made them
very small.   Then he tumbled them over the wall
into the ogre's garden.   And they crawled through a
hole in the garden fence and both ran home, Roger
one way and Hurricane the other, and neither dared
tell the king nor anyone else where he had been, nor

what the ogre had done to him. But it was two or three days before they became large again.

Then the king sent out some men with a cannon to batter down the walls of the ogre's castle. But the ogre sat on the wall and caught the cannon balls in his hand and tossed them back at the cannon, so that they broke the wheels and scared away all the men. And when the cannon sounded the ogre roared so loudly that all the windows in the king's palace were broken, and the queen and all the

The ogre tumbled them over the wall.

princesses went down into the cellar and hid among the sugar barrels, and stuffed cotton in their ears till the noise should stop. And whatever the king's men tried to do the ogre made it worse and worse.

And at last no one dared to go out into the valley beside the ogre's castle, and no one dared look at it from anywhere, because when the ogre scowled all who saw him dropped to the ground with fear, and

The queen and princesses hid in the cellar.

their teeth began to fall out, and when the ogre roared there was no one who could bear to hear it.

So the king and all his men hid in the cellar of the castle with the queen and the princesses, and they stuffed their ears full of cotton, and the ogre scowled and roared and had his own way.

But there was one little boy named Pennyroyal,

who tended the black horse Hurricane, and he was
not afraid of anything because he was a little boy.
And the little boy said he would go out and see the
ogre and tell him to go away. And they were all
so scared that they could not ask him not to go. So
Pennyroyal put on his hat, filled his pockets with
marbles and took his kite under his arm, and went
down the valley to the castle of the ogre. The ogre
sat on the wall and looked at him, but the little boy
was not afraid, and so it did the ogre no good to

"May I come in?" said Pennyroyal.

scowl. Then Pennyroyal knocked on the ogre's
door, and the ogre opened it and looked at the little boy.

"Please, Mr. Ogre, may I come in?" said Penny-

6

royal; and the ogre opened the door, and the little
boy began to walk around the castle looking at all
the things. There was one room filled with bones,
but the ogre was ashamed of it, and did not want to
let the little boy see it. So when Pennyroyal was

There was one room filled with bones.

not looking the ogre just changed the room and
made it small, so that instead of a room full of
bones it became just a box of jackstraws. And the
big elephant he had there to play with he made into
a lap-elephant, and the little boy took it in his hand
and stroked its tiny tusks and tied a knot in its trunk.

And everything that could frighten the little boy the ogre made small and pretty, so that they had great times together.

And by and by the ogre grew smaller and smaller, and took off his ugly old face with the long teeth and bushy eyebrows and dropped them on the floor and covered them with a wolf-skin. Then he sat down on the wolf-skin and the little boy sat down on the floor beside him, and they began to play jackstraws with the box of jackstraws that had been a room full of bones. The ogre had never been a boy himself, so jackstraws was the only game he knew how to play. Then the elephant he had made small snuggled down between them on the floor. And as they played with each other, the castle itself grew small, and shrank away until there was just room enough for them and for their game.

Up in the palace, when the ogre stopped roaring, the king's men looked in and saw that the ogre's castle was gone. Then Roger, the king's son, called for Pennyroyal. But when he could not find the boy, he saddled the black horse Hurricane himself and rode down the valley to where the ogre's castle had been. When he came back he told the king that the ogre and his castle were all gone. Where

the castle stood there was nothing left but a board
tent under the oak tree, and in the tent there were
just two little boys playing jackstraws, and between
them on the ground lay a candy elephant.

Just two little boys and a candy elephant.

That was all. For the terrible ogre was one of
that kind of ogres that will do to folks just what
folks do to him. There isn't any other kind of
ogre.

THE LEPRECHAUN AND THE FIELD OF GOLD.

ACROSS the sea on the Green Island there lives a little man they call the Leprechaun. He is a queer little fellow, not as big as Santa Claus, and though he is Santa Claus's brother the two do not look one bit alike. For the Leprechaun wears the finest of clothes, red coat, green vest, white trousers, and shoes "that for the shine of them would shame a looking-glass." He never sits down except when his shoes need polishing, and then he whips them off and gives them a rub up and down with a mullein leaf, and this makes them all right again. He does not wear a long beard like Santa Claus, but he has a high pointed hat, and he sticks the point of it into the ribs of folks that trouble him, and then they are tickled so that they can not do anything but just laugh and let him alone. The Leprechaun hates all girls because he is so little, and girls always like the big boys best. And he hates all school teachers, too, and in this he is right, for the school teachers on the

Green Island all say that there isn't any such person as a Leprechaun, just as the school teachers with us say that there isn't any such a man as Santa Claus; but if there wasn't any Santa Claus, how could the Leprechaun be his brother?

If you are looking for the Leprechaun, you will never find him, and that is why the school teachers think that there isn't any such thing, for they are always looking out for him. But children can find him, and the best place to look is among the berry bushes by the side of the ditch, when the sunshine is warm, and where he won't get the shine off his shoes when he is looking for berries. Then if you see him with his shoes off you can catch him, but you must never take your eyes off from him, either before or after you have him in your hands. You must never mind what he says, and you must follow him through the ditch, into the mud or among the berry bushes, anywhere he goes. If you take your eyes off from him you will never see him again so long as you live. It does not matter how wet or dirty you get your clothes if you only catch him. For he can tell you where the gold is, and if you can hold him long enough, and do not let him get into his shoes again, all the gold in the world is yours.

But you have to be very careful in dealing with him, even after you get him. They say that Tom O'Donovan once caught a Leprechaun and made him show the right place to dig for gold. It was almost night when the Leprechaun brought him to the place where the gold was hidden. So Tom set a stick in the ground and hung his old hat on it to mark the spot. The old hat had the rim loose on the front so that Tom could look right out through it. When he came back in the morning, the whole country was covered with sticks set up and an old hat on every one, and every hat had the rim loose in front, hanging down so that if the stick had eyes it could look out through the rip in the rim. And Tom could not tell which was his own hat, so he never knew which stick to dig under. All he got for his gold was a cartload of old hats. And his family have been wearing these old hats ever since, and they will never, never get them all worn out.

One day a little boy saw the Leprechaun picking berries by the side of the ditch. So he stepped up very softly behind and grabbed the little man and carried him up on the bank, holding him by one leg just as he used to hold his sister's doll. The Leprechaun scratched and screamed and screeched with all

his might, but the little boy would not let him go.
And he wouldn't take his eyes off from him either, so
the Leprechaun couldn't help himself at all. "Now
tell me where the gold is," said the little boy. "Let
me go first," said the Leprechaun. But the boy
would not, and squeezed him very hard. "How can
I find the gold," said the Leprechaun, "if you won't
let me walk?" "Let me tie you up first," said the
boy, and he took a string out of his pocket and tied
it into the Leprechaun's red belt with the golden
buckle on it. "When I find the gold, will you let
me go?" said the Leprechaun. And the boy said
he would.

Then the little man started off over the hills, and
the boy held him by the string and never took his
eyes off from him. And they went across the moss of
the bog and the rocks of the hill and through the
woods and down the stream till they came to a big
meadow, when the sun shone bright and warm and
the yellow buttercups stood thick in the tall grass.

"Here is the gold for you," said the little man.
"Where, where?" said the boy, for he wanted lots
of gold to buy candy and toys and fireworks, and he
wanted to get it as quick as he could.

"Why, all around you; just look," said the Lep-

rechaun.   But all the boy saw was the yellow buttercups shining in the sun.

Then the little boy said, "That isn't the right
kind of gold.   I want money gold; I want to buy
candy.   Give me money gold, and then you can go
where you want to."

"Oh, is that all?" said the Leprechaun; "you do
not want gold at all, but just candy.   If my gold is
not good for you, you can't have any gold of any
kind.   If you want just candy, you had better go
and find Santa Claus."

Then the little boy shut his eyes and began to
cry.   And the Leprechaun whisked off his belt and
slipped away as spry as a monkey, and sat down on
the bank and rubbed off his shoes with a mullein
leaf.   Then a cloud came before the sun and all the
buttercups were closed, so that there wasn't any more
gold, and it wouldn't buy candy if there were any.
And the little boy walked home alone through the
green grass, and he will never see the Leprechaun
again so long as he lives, and all because he wanted
the wrong kind of gold, and because when he was
looking for it he took his eyes off the little man and
let him get away.

THE POOKA AND THE LEPRECHAUN.

(With acknowledgments to D. A. McAnally.)

IN the Green Island the Pooka used to live. You would have thought that he was a horse from the looks of him, but there was never a saddle nor bridle on him, and he never shed his hair as real horses do. And at night when he went clattering, clattering down the road the fire flamed out of his nostrils so that he could see the way, and his eyes were red as fire, too. People who looked him in the eye saw that he was no real horse, but the Pooka, and so they were afraid.

For when the Pooka found anybody on a road alone at night, he would speak to him just like a man, and a nice and civil man too, asking him the time of night and the way to town, and talking about the weather, and all that. Then, if the man looked tired, he would ask him to ride on his back, as he was going his way. But when any one gave the Pooka a chance, the beast would grab him by the collar and

80

throw him on his back—and then what a ride he would have!

Up the hill and down the dale the Pooka would go, into the bogs, through the woods, and leaping over the rocks. And the man would hang on to the Pooka's mane with both hands, while the Pooka would kick up his heels; and by the light of his nostrils the rider would see all sorts of horrid things—spooks and dragons and goblins and were-wolves—so that he was just as afraid of falling off as he was of the Pooka. And when it was morning, the Pooka would shake the rider off anywhere he happened to be. Into the ditch he would fall, and there he would lie till somebody came along and picked him up. And sometimes it would take the man a month to find his way home again. So the people of the Green Island got very tired of having the Pooka roaming about all night, and never shedding his hair as a decent horse should. It was not nice to have him all the time talking to people just as civil as if he was an old friend, and then taking them off no one knows where.

Men say that the old king Brian Boru, who ruled over the Green Island a long time ago, once caught the Pooka and taught him better manners,

and made him shed too, just like any common
horse.

Once on a time the king went out into the great
woods when the Pooka had been running about, and
found a long black hair from the Pooka's tail sticking to a blackberry bush. And with this he made
some magic. I can not tell how he did this, because
I have never been a king, and only a king knows
what a king can do.

Then one night the king put the magic in his
pocket and walked out in the dark to see if he
couldn't find the Pooka.   And when he came out into
the big woods, he heard the hoofs clattering, clattering along, and he saw fire shine out from the nostrils and eyes.   Pretty soon the Pooka came along as
civil as you please. The king said, "Good evening,
Pooka!" and the Pooka said, "How do you do,
king?" And the king said that it was a fine warm
night, and the Pooka asked the king where he was
going.

Then when they had walked together arm in arm
for some time, talking about all sorts of things, the
king began to get tired. And the Pooka asked him
if he wouldn't like to ride with him, as they were both
going the same way. But the king said, "I would

came to the bottom of the hill. But the next day Diogenes thought he had had enough of that, so he got a lot of big hooked nails and nailed them all over the outside of his tub. Then when the bad boys came to roll him down the hill, their clothes caught in the hooked nails and they went rolling along with the tub and with Diogenes. When they had gone ka-bump! ka-bump! ka-bump! to the bottom of the hill, Diogenes came out of his tub and looked for the bad boys, and there they were all pressed out flat just like pancakes, and they weren't much thicker than wall-paper. So Diogenes gathered them up, and got some mucilage, and papered his tub inside and out with the flattened-out bad boys. Ever since then the bad boys of Corinth have gone to the other side of the town whenever they want to have a little fun.

HOW WE CAPTURED TROY.

(After an Ancient Document.)

THERE once were some Trojans, of course,
  So we Greeks built a big wooden horse;
    How Achilles did grin
    As we boys clambered in,
And he said, "How is this for a horse?"

We painted the beast black and red,
And Achilles he waggled its head,
    While behind for a tail
    Nestor's whiskers did trail,
But we might have used pea straw instead.

Then we fixed up four legs for the horse,
And they made me a fore-leg, of course,
    With Epeus and Pyrrhy
    And Patsy O'Leary,
We trotted him round on his course.

We tied the great horse to a tree,
Then the Trojans all came out to see;
134

like to ride, but I am afraid you are shedding and I would not want to get horsehairs all over my clothes."

But the Pooka said, "I am no common horse, I never shed, and you will never get one of my hairs on you, for all my hair is magic and it is all part of me."

"Is that so?" said the king. Then the king told his companion how nice it was to be young and strong as the Pooka was. "I have heard of you for many years," he said, "but I had no idea how young you were; you don't seem to be more than four years old. I never saw a grown-up horse before that looked so young."

"How old do you think I am?" said the Pooka. "Why, that is hard to tell," said the king; "but if you will open your mouth and let me look at your teeth, maybe I can guess."

So the Pooka laughed and opened his mouth very wide to let the king guess how old he was. Then the king took his magic out of his pocket and jammed it down the Pooka's throat, and the horsehair in it became an iron bit, and the rest of the magic became a stout wire bridle.

Then the king leaped on the Pooka's back, and away they went! The Pooka jumped and kicked and spurted fire from his nose, but it was no use. Away he had to go, and away the king went with him, and drove him wherever he would. And when the Pooka stopped the king would lash him with the long end of his wire bridle and prick him with his spurs till his hair came loose and he began to shed just like any other horse. This was because the magic was coming out of him, for when the magic is out of a Pooka he is just a plain, common horse.

Then the king rode him up to a steep hill that stood all alone in the woods between two mountains. And around and around this hill he made the Pooka canter up to the very top. Then he galloped down the same way, then right back up again, and so on, up and down all night.

When morning came the king and the Pooka had made a regular road like a corkscrew clear around the hill, and from bottom to top and from the top to the bottom. And the hill is there to this day, and they call it the Pooka Hill, and if you ever go to the Green Island you will see it just where the king and the Pooka left it, unless you happen to be looking for something else.

When it was daylight the king rode the Pooka home and he was all tamed, and ever since then he has shed his hair, just as he ought to, every fall and spring.

After that time when the Pooka finds a man on the road at night he never says a word to him, unless the man is lying in the ditch. If he is, then the Pooka picks him up and gives him a ride all over the country; but wherever he goes, he must bring the man back at daylight and leave him in the very same ditch where he found him. And sometimes the man who sleeps in the ditch never really rides at all, but just dreams of the Pooka. Then when he wakes up he does not know whether he has been on the Pooka's back or not, unless he finds some Pooka hairs on his clothes. If he does that, there is magic in them, and some day the Pooka will come back and give him another ride. If he doesn't want another ride, he must change his clothes. That is why men who fall to sleep in the ditches always wear old ragged clothes, and they always leave them there by the side of the road if they find any Pooka hairs on them.

One night the Pooka came along and found a Leprechaun by the side of the ditch with his shoes off, rubbing them up and down with a mullein leaf.

It was not a real ditch, for the Leprechaun has

magic in his shoes, and wherever you find him he is
sitting on the side of some ditch and around him
the briars grow and wild roses.   And all this is
there whether any ditch is really there or not.

So the Pooka came along and the Leprechaun
was brushing his shoes, just as he always does.
And they both said good-evening, just as civil as
they knew how.   But after they had talked awhile
the Pooka reached over and took the Leprechaun
in his teeth and threw him over on his back.   Then
he cantered away, and the Leprechaun hung to his
mane and away they went.   All night long they
clattered down the road, but when the Pooka came
to bring the Leprechaun back to where he came
from the ditch wasn't there.   And he looked for
it up and down the road everywhere, but he never
found it.   It was a magic ditch, and there was more
magic in the Leprechaun than there was left in the
Pooka after the king rode him so hard.

And so the Pooka could never put the Leprechaun where he found him, and he can never put him
down at all.   And there they are.

And on dark nights when the rain is falling, when
men hear the clatter of hoofs and see the fire flash
in the dark, they know that it is the Pooka with the

Leprechaun on his back hunting for the ditch where the little man came from. And till he finds it he cannot take anybody else on his back, and those who fall asleep in the ditch can lie there till morning, and then they needn't look for Pooka hairs on their clothes.

(With acknowledgments to Jacob Grimm.)

ONCE there was a prince, and he heard that a princess had been stolen away and carried to a far-off castle, and was kept shut up there, and

A whole lot of ghosts running up and down.

guarded with dragons. This prince had had a great deal of trouble because he was not afraid of any-

88

thing, and had never known how to shiver. He
never knew what shiver meant, and he wanted
to know what everything meant, so he felt very
badly about it. When he was told what terrible

He pinned his dagger through each one of them.

things there were around this princess he said he
would go and get her out, and maybe something
would make him shiver.

So he started out and by and by he came to the
castle wall, and outside the wall of the castle he saw
a band of ghosts running up and down, clanking
their chains. Then he took out from his belt his
dagger of illusion and pinned it through each one of
them, then stuck it into the wall, and the ghosts
could not help themselves, for they were not used to
being treated in that way.

Then he went on a little farther, and he found a great dragon with its mouth wide open and very ferocious. So he took a little double spear that he had with pointed barbs on both ends. He held the spear in one hand and thrust it sidewise into the dragon's mouth. Then he shut the two jaws of the dragon together with the other hand, and fastened them with the barbs of the spear, so that the dragon could not open his mouth; then the dragon, of course, had nothing more to do. Then he went on a little farther and found a great octopus reaching out his feelers in all directions—cold, clammy feelers, with sticking places all along them from one end to the other. So he took his knife and cut off a lot of feelers and rolled them into a bundle and held the bundle out among the others. And all the other feelers grabbed these and held on to them with all their might. So the prince went along without any trouble.

Then he went on a little farther until he came to a great hornets' nest full of hornets, and the hornets came out buzzing in every direction. The prince had on a great iron coat of mail and the hornets stuck their stings into the coat of mail and couldn't get in any farther, and by and by they got tired of trying to

sting iron. Just then the white woman who was
guarding the inside of the castle came out, and the
hornets left the prince and all took hold of her and

He came to a great hornets' nest.

stung her full of stings, and when they flew away the
stings held on, so they carried her off with them to
the clouds.

Then the prince went into the inside room of the
castle where the princess was. "Good evening,
princess," he said, and she replied, "Good evening,
prince." Then he asked her if she wouldn't like to

go out for a walk, but she said the white woman
wouldn't let her. The prince said he didn't think
the white woman would care this time, and when
they sent to ask her they couldn't find her. So they
went out for a walk in the garden of the castle.
They walked under the empty hornets' nest, and the

"Good evening, princess."

hornets were still flying away with the white woman
stung fast to their stings. They went by the octopus,
which was still wrestling with its own arms, holding
the old feelers fast with its own feelers. Next they
came to the old dragon, who was lying all in a heap
because he couldn't get his mouth open, for to open

his mouth and roar is all any dragon is good for. Then they came to the ghosts, who were still pinned tight to the wall with the dagger of illusion, which was the same sort of stuff they were made of, and so they couldn't help themselves. Then they went at last back to the prince's own home, because the prince said he didn't think the white woman would care any more, even if the princess never came back.

Then the prince and princess were married, and they had a great wedding, but the prince felt worse than ever because he had met all these horrible ghosts and dragons and things, and they had not all of them made him shiver once. So while he was sitting at the table at the dinner after the wedding the princess went out to a spring and dipped up a bucket of water and a lot of little cold cat-fishes. Then she came in and when no one was looking she poured all the cold fishes down the prince's back. Then the prince said " Ugh !" and they all laughed because he had learned how to shiver.

ONCE there was a little boy, and he wanted to be a ghost, so that he could see at night, and so he could climb up on the roof without having to hang on. So one night he woke up and found that he had his wish. He was a ghost, and he could see in the dark. And he went right up the chimney and out on the roof and slipped down the side of the house and out through the garden. There he stopped to think what he could do. For there wasn't anybody out in the garden for him to rush up to and say " Whoosh!" For that is what ghosts are always doing when there is any one around. He could not see anybody except the old cow, Jersey Lily, who was fast asleep under the oak tree, with the green alfalfa up to her chin. So the little boy who was a ghost glided up to the old cow and said " Whoosh !" The old cow opened her eyes and looked at him sleepily. Then the little boy remembered that ghosts sometimes take off their heads and

94

throw them at people. So he took off his head and threw it at the old cow, and it caught on her horns. The point of one horn went right into the ghost's eye. Then the cow saw that she had a ghost head stuck on her horn, and she was scared and began to bellow and run about and swing her tail terribly.

And the little boy ran after her, but he couldn't see in the dark any more because he hadn't any head with him. And the faster he ran the louder the cow bellowed and the more he couldn't get hold of his head. All at once the cow gave a great whoop, and turned round and ran right over him, and he grabbed at the head just as he tumbled over into the ditch with the old cow right on top of him. And when he had got his head back and put it on he lay right on the floor under the bed, and the bedclothes were all piled up over him, and his mother had turned on the electric lights so that she could see in the dark and find out what was the matter with the little boy.

THE OTTO-HEINRICH TOWER.

IN the Castle of Heidelberg in Germany there is a tall tower called the Otto-Heinrich Tower. In the top of this tower there is a window that has no glass in it. In the old days Prince Otto and Prince Heinrich lived together up in this tower. One day they had a quarrel and Heinrich threw Otto out

The Castle of Heidelberg.

through the window. Otto climbed around on the roof, where he was safe, but every little while he would try to come back through the window into the room, but Heinrich wouldn't let him. So he stayed there on the roof all that night and the next day. The tower was so high that his folks could not see him, and they did not know where to look for him.

Then he couldn't stand it any longer and he crawled around on the building until he got where he could drop down on the ground. And then, I suppose, he dropped down.

Many years have gone by since then, and Otto and Heinrich have both become ghosts. Now when people go up in that tower and sleep there, the first they know they will see somebody putting his head—a long, slim head, with bright yellow hair and burning eyes— around the outside of the window, try-ing to crawl in. If you let the head stay there, it will slam and push the window and fright-en you. If you

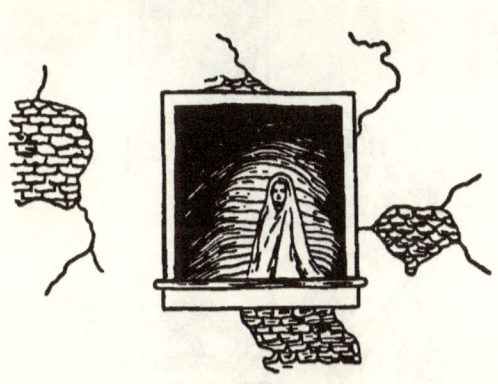

A long, slim head.

open the window, in comes the ghost of Prince Otto. Then you are very much scared and run down the stairs and the ghost runs after you. Down you go into the great hall below, where the fire is burning in the grate. But the minute the ghost comes into the draught, up the chimney he goes and comes out again on the outside of the tower.

One night somebody was sleeping there and he
wouldn't let Prince Otto in.   Then Otto slammed
the window so much that he shook it open, and hold-

You run down stairs and the ghost runs after you.

ing the window in front of him in his arms he chased
the man down the stairs.   Both of them ran very fast
and the ghost stumbled and fell, and the whole window pane crashed into atoms. ·Then he went up the
chimney and came out on the roof again, and now
since the window is gone he comes in and goes out

of the tower as he pleases. Nobody can stop him, and so nobody sleeps in the tower any more.

When the people are dancing down in the great room below and are having a good time, they look up at the ceiling, and all at once they see the face of Heinrich. He is a ghost too now, and down he comes from the ceiling, dropping like a football.

Up the chimney goes the ghost.

He bounds around on the floor, and then his teeth fall out, and if you pick them up you will find they are red-hot. Then the people are scared, and they all run out of the building, and Heinrich's ghost head goes bounding after them until it gets opposite the fireplace and then it goes up the chimney, just as the ghost of Otto does.

Nobody knows what Heinrich did to Otto in the

tower when he put him out the window, but it must
have been something very queer, to make their ghosts
act so. But you can see now in any picture of
Heidelberg Castle that there is no glass in the upper
window of the Otto-Heinrich Tower, and there will
never be any there.

WHY THE PARROT WAS SO STRONG.

(*With acknowledgments to Charles Lincoln Edwards.*)

ONCE all the animals could talk; the dogs could talk, and the cats and the owls and the rats and mice and chickens and the lion could talk—he is the king of beasts—and the elephant and all the rest of them. But when the children came they talked so much that the animals couldn't get a word in edgewise, and so they all gave up talking and attended to their other business. Only the parrot, he went off into the top of the tree and kept right on talking just the same, and one day when he sat in the top of the tree he said to himself: "I am the strongest animal there is in the world; I can pull harder than all the rest of them. There isn't one of them that can pull against me." Then the elephant heard it and he came out and motioned that he could pull harder than the parrot could. He had forgotten how to talk, but he wasn't going to let any animal brag of being stronger than he was.

101

So the parrot got a long rope and tied it to the elephant's front teeth and went back into the top of the tree and told the elephant when he said " Go ! " to pull with all his might, and he could pull harder than the elephant could.   Then the whale heard the parrot boasting of his strength and telling how hard he could pull.   So he came up and motioned that he could pull harder than any other animal.   Then the parrot said he was the strongest animal in the world, and would pull against the whale.   So he took the other end of the rope that wasn't hitched to the elephant and tied it around the whale's tail, and told the whale when he got all ready and said " Go ! " to pull with all his might.   So the parrot flew up into the top of the tree and said " Go ! " and then the whale pulled with all his might, and the elephant pulled with all his might too, and they pulled and pulled, and they pulled till the elephant's front teeth were drawn away out long, and they pulled till the whale was spread out so that he looked like a fish.   Then they pulled and pulled till by and by the rope broke close up to the elephant's teeth, and then the whale tumbled down with a great splash into the sea.   Then he couldn't get back on the shore at all, and ever since he has had to live in the sea just like a fish.

Then the elephant claimed that he had beaten the parrot, and the whale thought that he had beaten the parrot too.   When the whale came up to the shore and tried to tell the parrot that he was the strongest he had so much water in his nose that he had to blow it off with a great splash, and then the parrot and everybody else ran away, and there wasn't any-body that the whale could talk to, even if he hadn't forgotten how to talk.   Now whenever the whale comes to the top of the water he tries to say that he was the strongest, but all he can do is to blow the water out of the top of his nose.   And ever since then the elephant has gone around with a long piece of rope fastened to the front of his head just above his teeth, and the parrot talks away to himself and says that he is the king of birds, and no other bird can say that he is not.   For all the other birds have forgotten how to talk.

THE LOST XENIA.

(With acknowledgments to Edward Everett Hale.)

ONCE there was a sleeping car and its name was Xenia, and they painted the name in big red letters on the sides, XENIA, so that they wouldn't forget it. And the Xenia ran with the other cars over the mountains, and once they put it at the very end of the train.

On the mountains is a big curve they call the Horse-Shoe Bend, where the road winds away around so as to go up to the head of a gully that is too deep to build a bridge across.

So one day the train came down the mountain toward the Horse-Shoe Bend, puffing and thundering along, and the Xenia was the last car. And there was a little boy in the Xenia that had a red cap on, and there was the candy-boy, who had his basket full of peanuts. And there were lots of other people there and the porter, but they were grown-up people, so it does not make much difference who they were.

And the engine came thundering down the grade, and the engineer saw that there was a cow lying down on the track on the Horse-Shoe Bend. He couldn't stop the train, and he had to do something. So he steered the train to the right, and put on all the steam, and straightened out the engine's hind legs, so that she left the track, and gave a great jump into the air. And all the train came jumping into the air behind her. And they sailed along finely, just like a kite. Then the engineer steered the engine very carefully, and when she came down again she fell right on the track on the other side of the gully. They had gone straight across the bend and were all right on the other side, and the cars came right after the engine, and they went thundering along down the side of the mountain.

But when the conductor came to go through the train he noticed that one car was gone. They couldn't find the Xenia anywhere, and the little boys and girls couldn't buy any peanuts, for the candy-boy was gone too.

And the conductor telegraphed back. And men went down into the gully and all through the woods about the Horse-Shoe Bend and hunted for the lost car, but they couldn't find it, and they haven't found it yet. Probably it is not there. But they don't know. All they know is that a few days later the men were looking at the great white moon through the big telescope at the Lick Observatory up on Mount Hamilton. Then they saw a dark-looking thing floating along above the moon. And it had some red letters on its sides. It was so far off they could not see just what it was. It seemed to be long with square corners, with shining places every little way, or maybe holes through it that showed the light. It was shaped some like a jew's-harp, but it must have been a good deal bigger, because they could see its shadow on the moon.

By and by it stopped on the white side of the moon, and little black things that looked no bigger than ants crawled out of it and walked around, and the men could see their black shadows on the silver-white moon. And one of the smallest ones had a red cap on. And one of the others had a basket, but it wasn't half full of peanuts, so that they don't know whether it is the same candy-boy or not, for the other candy-boy had his basket full. So it may be that this is not the lost Xenia after all. Maybe the Xenia broke loose from the train when it jumped and went on up through the air to the moon. But maybe she didn't, and just ran off the track and got off on some other railroad, and was mixed up with the other cars. But if you find on any railroad any-where a car named *Xenia*, you will know that it is the car that got away. Then you will write to Mr. Pullman at Chicago, Illinois, and tell him about it. For he has worried a good deal about the Xenia and what has become of her, and he has been sorry to lose the candy-boy. So he will be very glad to know what has become of this car, and he will tell the candy-boy to give you all the peanuts you can eat.

The lost car and the moon.

ONCE the Trojans had a big city with a wall all around it, and they called it Troy. The Greeks wanted to get in and take the city, but they could not do it. So they stayed outside and tried every way they could think of, but they couldn't get in. So the captain of the Greeks had them build one night a great big wooden horse, and when they had built the horse he got inside of it and moved its head up and down just like a real horse, and he put four men into its legs to make it walk. Then old Nestor, who was the oldest man in the world in those days, got inside the horse, and his long whiskers reached out behind for a tail. And all the rest of the Greeks crawled into the inside of the horse and shut the door. So they walked the horse all around the city, and then tied it to a tree. In the morning, the Trojans looked out from the gates of Troy and saw a big wooden horse hitched to a tree, and nobody around. So they went out and unhitched the horse and led him into Troy, and tied him to a tree in the park, and gave him hay to eat, and were very much delighted to get such a fine beast for nothing. And when it came night and the Trojans had all gone to sleep, the captain of the Greeks crawled out of the horse's neck, and Nestor

The wooden horse.

crawled out of the horse's tail, and all the rest out of its body, just leaving one man in each leg. Then the Greeks went all through Troy, and caught all the people when they were fast asleep, and stowed them away inside of the horse. When they got them all laid away, they led the horse out through the city gate and turned him loose outside of the city with all the Trojans inside of him. The Trojans woke up in the morning very much surprised, because they hadn't expected anything of this kind. They did not know what to think about it, and they believe to this day that the horse got loose in the night and ate them all up, and then ran out through the city gate, and that the Greeks came in through the city gate that they had left open when the horse ran away.

THERE once was a couple of bears
  Who were eating baked apples on shares.
  When the apples were gone
  They ambled along
In search of a dish of baked pears.

THE DANCING SHADES.

ONCE there was a pretty little girl, her name was
Eurydice, and she had gone down to the Under
World to be a Shade. Her brother Orpheus felt very
badly about it, and by and by he found out where
the hole was that led down to
the place where the Shades
stay. So he brought out his
fiddle and took in one hand a
piece of bread dipped in the
magic honey they call hydromel,
the kind that the witch-bees of
Miletus make, and in the other
hand he took a piece of money.
Then he started down through
the hole to where the Shades
are. He went away down
through the long dark cave, and
then on to the place where the
river runs through. This river is called Styx, and
on this river is a ferryboat, and they call the ferry-

Eurydice.

man Charon, because he is always carrying Shades across the River Styx. Orpheus gave Charon his piece of money and Charon ferried him across. When he got across he found on the other shore a big three-headed dog that stands there, and this three-headed dog always barks at everybody that goes across the river. And one head has a big loud bark, and one a little squeaky bark, and the other bark is just regular like any other dog. Once they used to have three dogs there, but they ate a good deal, and there wasn't anything for the three bodies to do. So Charon broke the heads off and put them all on one body, and made a three-headed dog, and he named the dog Cerberus. So Orpheus broke off three pieces of the bread dipped in hydromel and gave one piece to each of the three heads of Cerberus. Then the three heads stopped barking and let him go by.

He went on farther and farther until he came to a big room where the Shades were. The Shades there were walking about, and being Shades they walked right through each other, because Shades can do that, for they haven't any bone in them nor any blood. Some of the Shades were sitting one above the other in the same chair. There were Shades lying down on the ground and some lying upon the roof, because they can lie on the ceiling just as well as anywhere else; and some were lying in the fire, because fire burns right up through them and doesn't hurt them. The flame of the fire is a Shade itself.

Orpheus looked all around to find the Shade of his little sister Eurydice. By and by he found her sitting on a mossy bank by the side of a pretty waterfall. So he gave her a piece of bread dipped in hydromel, and this magic honey cured her of being a Shade. So all at once she began to have flesh and bones and blood in her. Then she wasn't a Shade any more, and then she walked around on the ground just like Orpheus. And then Orpheus took out his fiddle and he played a funny old tune, one that the Shades all like, because they used to sing it when they were children.

When he began to play Orpheus began to dance and his sister clapped her hands in time, and then the Shades caught up the tune and began to sing and pat and jump around. When they began to dance and keep time they became alive again and soon had flesh and blood and bones in them. Then they all began to sing and pat, all in the same tune. And when they were all stirred up Orpheus left the Shade place and came out into the passage-

way, and all the Shades followed. Then they came
to the three-headed dog, and when the dog heard them
all the heads began to bark, " Wow, wow," in three
different keys, one high and loud, one little and
squeaky, and one just regular, as any other dog
would bark. Then they all came down to the river
and Charon began to dance and pat, and blood and
bones came into him, the boat began to jump about,
keeping time just the same, and the river began to
rise up in waves. Then they went along beyond the
river. Orpheus was first, and then Eurydice. Then
came the three-headed dog, then Charon and the boat
dancing along ; then after them followed all the rest
of the Shades, and the river bringing up the rear, all
going on dancing and patting to the old tune that the
Shades love so much. So they went along, and kept
on dancing and singing all the time until they came
out through the cave into the green fields of Miletus.
Then all the animals joined the line ; the cattle began
to keep time with their tails and their horns, and
the horses began to dance and the dogs began to
bark ; the trees kicked their feet loose and followed,
waving their long limbs all in time ; the tables ran
out of the houses, jumping up on their legs and
swinging their leaves, and everything else there was

came along too. By and by they came back into the town where the Shades all used to live. There were no people left there then, because they had all gone down to be Shades, but ever since there has been plenty of folks. The old town is full of people now, and whenever they get a chance they all dance along the road and pat and sing the old song of the Shades. And those who have fiddles play them with all their might.

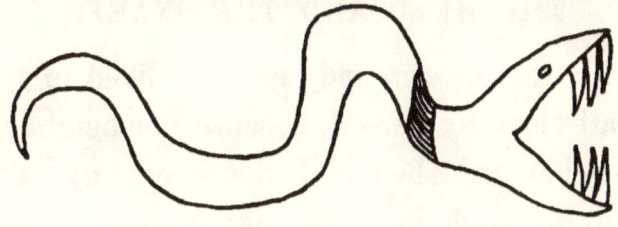

Medusa.

THE HEAD AND THE SNAKES.

ONCE there was a lady and she lived in a house all alone by herself, because her neighbors did not like her and she could not keep any servants. The trouble with her was that instead of hair she wore snakes, and her eyes turned everybody they looked on into stone, and whenever a tramp came along and knocked on the door and called for the lady of the house, she had only to look on him a moment and he turned into stone. She had in her back yard a whole pile of people leaned up against the fence, and every one of them had been turned into stone, because whenever she looked at anybody it turned him into stone.

The neighbors got very tired of her, and so they

told Perseus about it, and Perseus went off and borrowed a pair of wings that belonged to Quicksilver,* and he fastened them on his feet. Then he went around to Venus and borrowed a nice new looking-glass she had, and he took that in his left hand.

Medusa was taking a nap.

Then he went out and got his big broadsword and took that in his right hand. Then he flew away with the wings to the house where Medusa lived, but he did not dare look at Medusa for fear she

---

* "Quicksilver is the same as Mercury and sounds better" (*Knight*). Hawthorne has made a similar observation.

would turn him into stone, and he felt how ridicu-
lous he would look turned into stone, with wings
on his feet and a looking-glass in his hand! So he
walked on his toes backward up to the house and
knocked with his hind foot on the door. Nobody
came to the door, so he turned the knob and went in
backward. Now it happened that Medusa was taking a nap on the lounge, and there wasn't a single
serpent, by good chance. that was awake. So Perseus backed up to the lounge, holding the mirror before him, so that he could see where he was going,
until he was opposite her; then looking into the
mirror he swung his sword over backward and cut
Medusa' head right off, and then he grabbed it in
his hand by the frizzes of snakes and went right out
through the door without saying good-by or anything, and flew away with the head in his hand.

Then he did not know what to do with the head,
and the blood dripped out of it and fell into the sand,
and every drop that fell made a new snake, and the
track over the desert of Libya where he went has
been filled with snakes ever since, made out of that
blood. Finally he carried the head around to where
he saw a great big whale swimming after a girl that
somebody had tied to a rock out by the sea, and the

girl was crying and calling for her mother. So he
just turned the face of Medusa on the whale and

Perseus flies away with Medusa's head.

changed the whale into stone, and the whale lies there
and has been stone ever since. But the girl he
untied, and he showed her the way to go home. Still
Perseus did not know how to get rid of the head.
He never dared to look at it at all for fear it would
turn him into stone. Finally as he flew about on the
wings of Quicksilver, he saw old Jove taking a morning stroll through the skies, and he told Jove that he

9

might have the head if he wanted it for his museum. And Jove was much pleased, for he liked all sorts of odd things, and he took it from Perseus and hung it up on one of the stars, and there it hangs yet, and if you go out any night and look up into the sky you will see that head way off in among the stars. There are three stars of them making a triangle away on the other side of the North Pole from the

The girl tied to a rock, crying for her mother.

Big Dipper, and the star the head is fastened to is the one in the angle at the middle. And when the head

was hung up its face was turned toward the earth
and it changed the earth into stone, and that is why

Jove hangs Medusa's head on a star.

there is so much rock and stone on the earth now.
And some say that the moon was changed to stone
too. But I don't know about that; the moon looks
too white to be stone. Anyhow, up in the sky the old
head of Medusa is hanging yet, and if you go out at
night you want to look at it over your right shoulder.

ONCE there was a city and the people who lived there called it Thebes, because that was its name. One morning when the people got up they

The city gate and the Sphinx.

went out to the gate of the city; and they saw sitting by the gate a great big Sphinx that did not belong

122

to them, and they did not know whose Sphinx it was.

The Sphinx said, "It is all right. I will just sit here by the gate, and whenever any one comes into your city I will ask him a riddle. If he can guess that riddle, it is his good luck, he can go into the city. But if he doesn't guess it, I will eat him. In that way I will get enough to eat, and it will be perfectly just to every one, because if they don't guess the riddle it is only fair that I should eat them, and if they do guess it they can go into the city, and that will be all right too."

So when the gate was opened the Sphinx said to the first one that came: "Now answer me this riddle before you go any farther. What is it that walks on four legs in the morning, on two legs at noon, and on three legs at night?" The man could not think what it was, so he guessed a grasshopper, and the Sphinx said, "No, that is wrong." So she ate him. And of the next man that came along the Sphinx asked the same riddle, and he guessed it was a wheelbarrow, and the Sphinx said that was wrong. So she ate him. And then another man, and another man, and another man all came along, and they all guessed wrong, and the Sphinx ate them. And she

had so much to eat that she was getting quite fat—
for a Sphinx.

But one day there came along a man who was
lame, and who had hard work to get along over the

The Sphinx ate one man and then another.

stones. His name was Œdipus, and everybody
called him Ed. And the Sphinx said to Ed: "Answer me this riddle before you go any farther. Tell
me what it is that walks on four legs in the morning,
on two legs at noon, and on three legs at night."
And Œdipus said: "Why, anybody could guess that.

It's almost night now'; I am walking on three legs—
two legs and my cane; and when I was a baby it was
like morning to me, then I went on four legs; and
when I was a man before I was lame, it was like
being noon, and then I walked on two legs; now it
is night, I am lame and walk on three legs. So I am
the answer to your riddle." And the Sphinx said

The riddle.

thoughtfully: "I guess that's right; that's just about
the way I thought it out." And then Œdipus said:
"Now it's my turn to ask you a riddle. What have

you got inside your head?" Then the Sphinx said,
"Why, brains, I suppose. I will guess brains." But
Œdipus said, "No, that is wrong, you haven't any
brains at all; you have nothing in your head but
bread and milk." And the Sphinx saw there was

Perseus turned Medusa's head on the Sphinx.

only one way to find out which was right, and that
was to look and see. So Œdipus took his big cane
that had an axe on the upper end—for the people
used to wear axes on their canes in those days,
so that if they had to go to war they would be all

ready. Then he took his axe-cane and split open the Sphinx's head. They found that there were brains in there, just as the Sphinx had said; so Œdipus was wrong, and the Sphinx was quite right. But when they came to put the Sphinx together again they could not make her alive any way they tried, but they did not try very hard. Anyhow, she could not ask any more riddles nor eat any more folks. So when Perseus came along next day with the head of Medusa and saw the split Sphinx lying there, he just turned Medusa's face on her, and she was changed into stone. And, all turned into stone, she lies there yet with a split head, just outside the gates of the City of Thebes.

And the people were very thankful to Œdipus because he had got rid of the Sphinx for them; and so when he died they put witch-stuff all over him and wrapped him up in cloth and cloth and cloth, and made a mummy of him, and you can see him any day if you will go down to the museum.

ONCE there was a great bird with bright red feathers, just like a geranium or a flame of fire, and they called her Phœnix, because they couldn't think of any other name for such a queer-looking bird.

And one day the bird Phœnix flew right into the house, and made her nest in the grate, and laid a big round egg, all red, with little blue speckles over it. And the Japanese boy, Otaki, built a fire in the grate, and the fire burned the bird all up, and there wasn't anything left but the big egg, and that was red-hot, besides being red to begin with. And all at once the big egg went pop, and out flew the old bird Phœnix, just as she was before, with her red feathers and her old bill bent down in the middle, and her long blue spindling legs. And the children were playing camp out in the garden, where there was lots of yellow grass. And they gathered some of the grass to play they had a camp fire. And the old bird Phœnix made a nest right in the grass, and laid

128

a big red egg in it, all covered over with blue speckles. So the children lighted the camp fire with some matches they had, and burned the bird Phœnix all up, all but the red-hot egg. And the children felt very bad about it, because they thought that it was one of the big herons that fly over from the bay to catch gophers, but it wasn't, for the red egg went pop! and out flew the old bird Phœnix and lit on the eaves of the barn, just above the monkey's perch. Then John, the Swedish man, had been pruning the grape vines and had a great pile of limbs out on the ground by the pile of rocks. And the old bird Phœnix made her nest in it, and laid her egg just as she always did. And when John came to burn the brush, he burned her up too, and the egg went pop, and out she flew and lit on the very top of a live oak tree, and the wind was blowing so that she had to keep moving about with her long legs to keep from falling off. And the very next place she saw where there was going to be a fire she laid her egg. And one day Otaki saw her trying to scratch a match on the rough feathers on her knee, so as to make a fire to burn herself up. He didn't want any such bird as that around, so he drove her off. She flew around the world and away back up into history, for she could fly backward as well as forward with those long red wings of hers, and the long blue legs sticking out behind like a rudder.

She came to the palace where the Emperor lived, and he was a great fat Emperor and did nothing but eat. His real name was Heliogabalus, but the people called him Pig, because that was shorter and sounded more like him. And the Emperor Pig saw the bird Phœnix trying to build a nest in his cooking stove. And when he saw the egg he told his servants to wring the bird's neck, and make an omelet out of the egg, and to give him both the egg and the bird for his breakfast. So the Emperor Pig ate the old bird Phœnix and ate her egg too, and when the egg went pop, the people rushed in and saw that something had happened. There wasn't any Emperor left that they could find, and out of the chimney of the palace they saw a great red streak flying away, with long blue spindling legs following on behind. And she must be flying yet, for no one since that time has heard her eggs go pop! But if you should happen to see a big red egg lying in a brush-heap anywhere, build a fire under it, and maybe you will find the old bird Phœnix.

DIOGENES AND THE NAUGHTY BOYS.

(With acknowledgments to Fliegende Blätter.)

ONCE in the olden time there was a big city called Corinth, and at the upper end of the street there was a high hill, and on the hill there lived an old man named Diogenes. He didn't live in a regular house, but just in a big tub, a sort of a barrel, and he had a lot of straw inside where he used to sleep, and he had a lantern too, and he used to walk around at night in the streets looking for an honest man. But he never found any, because he was just pretending, and he looked the other way when he saw an honest man coming. The bad boys of Corinth followed him home one night, and he lay down in his tub and went to sleep, and when he was fast asleep the bad boys took the barrel and rolled it down the hill. Diogenes went rumble-de-bump! rumble-de-bump! till the barrel came clear down to the bottom of the hill. Then he got out, and he was pretty mad, but the bad boys were all gone and there wasn't any light in his lantern, and the

matches were all scattered in the straw.   So he rolled
his barrel back to the top of the hill.

The next night he went to sleep again, and the

The tub in which Diogenes lived.

1. It is on the hill.   3. Diogenes drove some nails in the tub.
2. The bad boys pushed it down the hill.   4. The boys were pressed into pancakes.

bad boys came and rolled him down the hill again,
and   he   went   r-r-r-le-bump !   le-bump !   till   he

But never a squeak
Did they hear from a Greek,
"All aphone now," says Nestor, says he.

Then the Trojans all chortled for joy
As they led the great horse into Troy,
　　But the Greeks hid within
　　Lay all silent as sin,
For we would not surprise or annoy.

To a big poplar tree in the park
They tied the great horse just at dark;
　　They called him Old Charley,
　　And gave him some barley,
That he might not be biting the bark.

Then they locked up the great city gate,
And before the town clock had struck eight,
　　They were all safe in bed,
　　For every one said,
"'Tis time to re–cu–perate."

When Sleep spread her wings over Troy
And Hypnos her arts did employ,
　　Then from out the great horse,
　　We Greeks crawled, of course,
And we reddened the town in our joy.

10

While the Trojans still peacefully slept,
In their chambers we stealthily crept,
   And each Trojan, of course,
   We removed to the horse,
Then the bolt through its fastening slipped.

When the Trojans were all stowed inside,
Said Achilles, "Now give them a ride!"
   Through the great city gate
   The horse started straight,
And we left him alone in his pride.

Then Achilles, he led us on foot,
To the sign of the "Horns of the Goat,"
   Then to Bacchus did homage,
   With incident damage
To the skins at the Inn of the Goat!

Thus the long night wore wearily on
Till it came to its end with the dawn,
   When eager-lipped Eos
   Kissed snow-mantled Chios
And awakened Aurora the Dawn.

Then the Trojans got up, rubbed their eyes,
And each said, "Well, this *is* a surprise.

I was safe in my bed,
But now I've been fed
To this monster in equine disguise."

And the Trojans believe, to this day,
That the beast which thus bore them away
    Had got loose in the night,
    For it was not tied tight,
And had swallowed them all in his play!

THE EAGLE AND THE BLUE–TAILED SKINK.

THERE was once a Blue-tailed Skink, and he sat on a log in the sun and had a good time, and on top of the tree over his head there was a big bald Eagle. The Eagle watched the Blue-tailed Skink sitting on the log in the sun until she thought it was time to eat him. Then she swooped down on him. When the Blue-tailed Skink saw the Eagle coming he gave a jump forward, so that when the Eagle got down there she just caught the

The Eagle swoops down on the Skink.

end of his tail. The tail of the Blue-tailed Skink will come off if you catch hold of it. It is made and put on that way. So the Blue-tailed Skink left the Eagle with the tail in her claws. He was all right himself, and he ran down the side of the log while the Eagle ate up the tail.

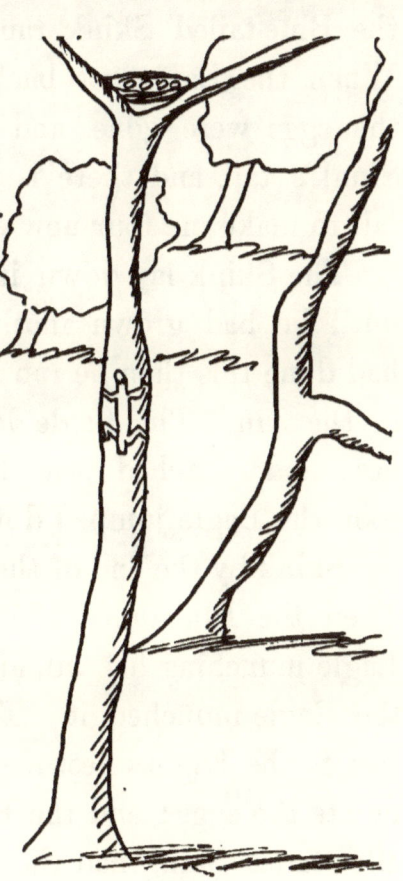

The Skink goes up the tree for the eggs.

Then the Blue-tailed Skink looked up the tree and saw where high in the crotch of the tree the Eagle had a nest. In the nest were four eggs. So the Blue-tailed Skink ran up the side of the tree to the nest. Then he looked down and saw the Eagle on the log eating up his tail. So he ate up the four eggs that the Eagle had laid in her nest, and he said, " There is just enough meat in these eggs to make me a new tail."

The Eagle saw the Blue-tailed Skink sitting in the nest on the tree, so she flew up to seize him. But the Blue-tailed Skink ran down on the other side. When the Eagle got back to her nest she saw that the eggs were gone, and she said, "I've eaten the Skink's tail, and there is just enough meat in that tail to make me four new eggs."

The Skink lay down in the shade under the log until he had grown another blue tail, and when he had done this then he ran back up on the log and sat in the sun. The Eagle laid four more eggs in the nest and watched the Blue-tailed Skink. Very soon the Eagle jumped down to catch him. She got the Skink by the end of the tail and the tail came off. Then the Blue-tailed Skink ran away and saw the Eagle munching his tail, and the tail squirmed while the Eagle munched it. Then the Skink ran up the tree to the Eagle's nest and saw four eggs there. So he ate the eggs; and the Eagle had the tail and the Blue-tailed Skink had the eggs, and they were ready to start over again. For there was meat enough in the tail to make four more eggs, and meat enough in the eggs to make another blue tail.*

* "The blue-tailed Skink never lost his tail forever."—BARBARA.

THE SEA HORSE AND THE LITTLE SEA PONIES.

HE was a little bit of a sea horse, and his name was Hippocampus. He was not more than an inch long, and he had a red stripe on the fin on his back, and his head was made of bone, and it had a shape just like a horse's head, but he ran

The sea horse hangs by his tail from seaweed.

out to a point at his tail, and his head and his tail were all covered with bone. He lived in the Grand Lagoon at Pensacola in Florida, where the water is shallow and warm and there are lots of sea-weeds. So he wound his tail around a stem of sea-

wrack and hung with his head down, waiting to see
what would happen next, and then he saw another
little sea horse hanging on another seaweed. And
the other sea horse put out a lot of little eggs, and
the little eggs all lay on the bottom of the sea at
the foot of the seaweed. So Hippocampus crawled
down from the seaweed where he was and gathered
up all those little eggs, and down on the under side
of his tail where the skin is soft he made a long slit
for a pocket, then he stuffed all the eggs into this

Each egg hatched out a little sea pony.

pocket and fastened it together and stuck it with
some slime. So he had all the other sea horse's eggs
in his own pocket.

Then he went up on the seawrack again and
twisted his tail around it and hung there with his
head down to see what would happen next. The
sun shone down on him, and by and by all the little

eggs began to hatch out, and each one of the little eggs was a little sea pony, shaped just like a sea horse. And when he hung there with his head down he could feel all the little sea ponies squirming inside his pocket, and by and by they squirmed so much that they pushed the pocket open, and then every one crawled out and got away from him, and he couldn't get them back, and so he went along with them and watched them to see that nothing should hurt them. And by and by they hung themselves all up on the seaweeds, and they are hanging there yet. And so he crawled back to his own piece of seawrack and twisted his tail around it and waited to see what would happen next. And what happened next was just the same thing over again.

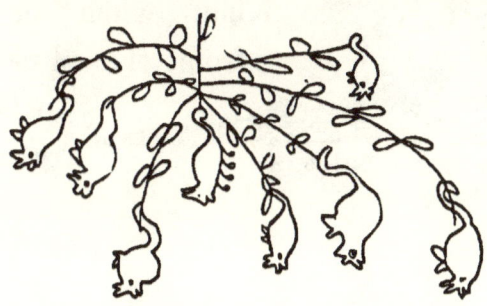

I.

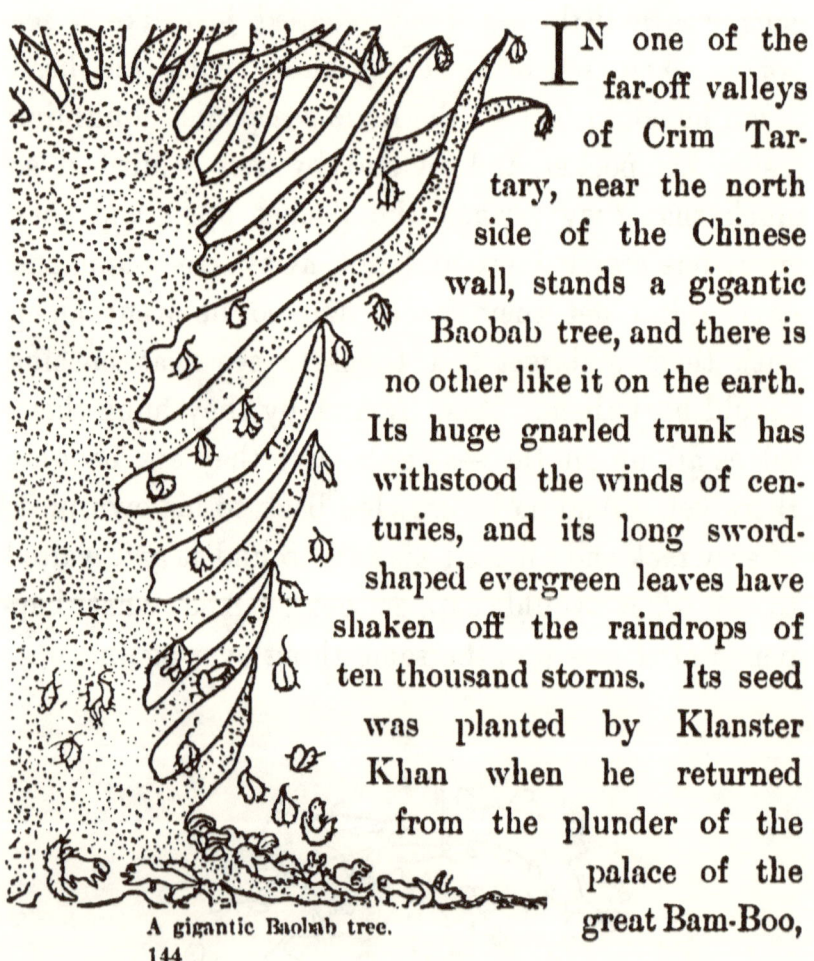

IN one of the far-off valleys of Crim Tartary, near the north side of the Chinese wall, stands a gigantic Baobab tree, and there is no other like it on the earth. Its huge gnarled trunk has withstood the winds of centuries, and its long sword-shaped evergreen leaves have shaken off the raindrops of ten thousand storms. Its seed was planted by Klanster Khan when he returned from the plunder of the palace of the great Bam-Boo,

A gigantic Baobab tree.

144

and rested with his army in the valley of Quong-Sin-Lee. And now the tree has grown great, and it lives long after the palace and the army have been alike forgotten.

Once, and once only, in a century the Baobab tree is covered with blossoms which draw the birds and the bees from a hundred provinces. The dark green of its foliage is relieved by large bell-shaped flowers with snowy white petals, a little yellowish in the center and dappled with a rich purple, as if each flower had been splashed with blood. A strange heavy odor exhales from the flowers,—an odor as of bumblebees among clover blooms,—and in the warm sunshine the odor grows stronger, like the smell of the incense which is burned in the temple of Joss. When the tree is in full bloom the whole valley is filled with fragrance. But this lasts only for a day. The warm winds blow up from the desert, the white petals wither, and the tree is once more a mass of dark glistening green. But the little fruits are left hidden among the leaves, and in the month of the tea harvest they become ripe. Each fruit is then a great, pitcher-shaped pod, long and narrow in the neck, short and rounded in the bowl, and its skin is hard like the rind of a gourd. When the fruits are ripe they fall to the ground, and the shock splits the shell into five long strips. Each one of these curls itself up convulsively, casting the pulp of the fruit far out on the ground. This pulp soon assumes a singular form. It is more like an animal than a plant. It has the power of motion, and its movements are as vigorous as those of a brownie. Should you see one, you would know it at once to be that curious creature called in books of science the Griffin.

And singular though the Griffin is, the mode of its origin is still more curious. Some think it the natural product of the ripened fruit of the Baobab tree. This view was held by all the older botanists, like Rafinesque and Lagerstrom and the University of Abo. But many of the modern investigators, like Stiefelknecht, Pretzelfresser, and Abner, Dean of Angels, take a very different view. According to them, the Griffin is not a fruit of the Baobab tree at all. It is produced by the development of the egg of the Gryphos or Baobab vulture, which is found only in the valleys of Crim Tartary. This huge bird comes buzzing about the tree at its flowering time in early June, ostensibly in pursuit of bees, but in reality seeking a chance to plant its eggs in the flower, to leave its offspring, as it were, a foundling on the steps of this wonderful tree.

Be this as it may, the fact is well known that when the Baobab tree ripens its fruits, the ground is strewn with small Griffins which have escaped from its gourd-shaped pods. These baby Griffins, or Grifflets, are very active and restless, and they have a way of rushing together in twos or threes, so that a single one is seldom seen. Then by a remarkable process, just the opposite of that which naturalists call fission, these little clusters of two or three run into one, as raindrops run together when coursing down a window-pane. So from two or three small Grifflets is formed one larger one, and the process goes on up to the third day, when only a single Griffin is left as the sum of all the others. On the day our story begins, such a Griffin stood alone in the world beneath the Baobab tree. And so his life began.

II.

I can not tell in these few pages one half the story of the Griffin's wanderings. Time was nothing to him and space was little, and with every day he saw new scenes and met with fresh adventures. He had roamed far and wide over the earth, far away from Crim Tartary and the scenes of his youth. He had come among people who had never heard of Quong-

Sin-Lee, and to whom the Chinese wall and the great Baobab tree were less real than the lamp of Aladdin or the bean-stalk of Jack the slayer of giants.

The Griffin found himself one summer evening on the grass-grown sidewalk of a little country village. By his side was the Postage Stamp, and in a lively way she was telling him her adventures and those of her hundred sisters from whom she had never been separated. But as the sun was setting a great storm arose and the red glare of the lightning was fearful. The Postage Stamp drew close to the Griffin for protection, and when the rain began to fall she clung more closely still. Soon they reached the awning of the corner grocery, where, upon the postmaster's invitation, they sought shelter within. Seated on the bench by the stove, the Postage Stamp struggled to free herself, but in vain. And the stupid postmaster, simply noticing that the Griffin bore a stamp, and without waiting for any explanation, threw them together into the mail pouch. The pouch was flung into the mail wagon and carried to the station, where, amid the noise and tumult of the incoming train, the Griffin's struggles for release were unnoticed. So with the little Postage Stamp fast to

his side, he was unwillingly whirled away upon his
travels.

The situation was embarrassing to both these vic-
tims of official zeal. Try as they might, they could
not separate themselves without fatal injury to the
Postage Stamp; and as the Griffin was too well bred
to allow any harm to come to a lady in his care, he
seemed not to notice her confusion, and tried to cheer
her up by saying that he was glad in his travels to
be assured of such good company.

By and by the mail bag was opened, and its contents—letters, papers, photographs, Griffin and all—
were spread out on a large table in the moving car.
All the letters bore plain directions, and the postal
clerk had no difficulty in sending each to its proper
destination. But when he came to the Griffin,
who bore only a stamp and no direction, he was
puzzled. He could simply carry him to the end of his
route, and then turn him over to another clerk, who
did the same. And so from clerk to clerk the Griffin
went for several days. One of them tried to send him
to the Dead Letter Office, but the officers there
would not take him, for whatever he was, he was cer-
tainly not a dead letter; how can you make a dead
letter out of a live Griffin? Finally, one of the clerks

tied a large paper tag around the Griffin's neck and wrote these words upon the tag in large letters:

"TRY GRIFFIN'S MILLS, GEORGIA."

In the early dawn of a summer morning, Mr. Absalom Billingslea, postmaster at Griffin's Mills, opened his office after the Tallahassee Express had passed by. The mocking-birds sang in the Crape myrtles outside his window, and a little farther on the morning fogs hung white and heavy over Brushy Creek. Absalom Billingslea emptied the mail pouch on the counter, humming to himself the old refrain,

> " Georgia girls, there's none surpasses,
>   For they are fond of sorghum molasses,"

and proceeded to sort out the letters. He was a good man, but he had never been far outside of Spaulding County, and he had never seen a Griffin before. When this queer creature fell out on the counter among the letters and papers, Absalom Billingslea jumped back in astonishment, and before he had recovered himself the Griffin had escaped through the open door.

He was gone, and to this day Mr. Billingslea is not sure whether he really saw him, or whether some excellent peach brandy which he had taken the night before in company with Colonel Moses Grice had caused the apparition. The Griffin ran swiftly along the empty street down the hill toward Brushy Creek. A great fog-bank hung over the stream, looking like a snow-white mountain on which were neither houses nor people. Fear of capture gave the Griffin unusual speed, and soon he began to climb the white wall. Being an unreal animal, he had no difficulty in doing this, and within half an hour he was resting quietly on the top. He said some words of cheer to the Postage Stamp, and she soon recovered herself, and began to chat about her sisters and to wonder whether they missed her at home.

All too soon, however, the sun arose, and the mists which had come up in the night hastened back to their hiding places in the swamp. The fog-bank vanished, and in an instant the Griffin found himself struggling with the cold waters of Brushy Creek. He was a stout swimmer, and a few strokes brought him to the bank. But the Postage Stamp was not so fortunate. The sudden bath had loosened her hold on the Griffin. She had never learned to swim, and she soon drifted into the eddy, where a muffle-jaw and a dollardee were already struggling for her

11

possession. The conflict did not last long. The muffle-jaw put out his long under lip, his mouth opened wide, and in it went both the dollardee and

The Griffin grieves over the loss of the Postage Stamp.

the Postage Stamp together, and the Griffin saw them no more.

The Griffin was profoundly grieved by such an unhappy end to a pleasant acquaintance. He was, however, an unreal animal, and to such as he only unreal things seem real. This being a real calamity he soon forgot it. He ran briskly across the fields, farther and farther from the town. Finding a large flat stump, he climbed upon it and lay down to rest and dry in the sunshine. The squirrels gathered around at a respectful distance, the redbirds sang to him, the trumpet-flowers nodded, and everything seemed to say, " How good it is to be alive in May!"

But far above his head, in great circles, flew the turkey-buzzard, watching all his movements with

The turkey-buzzard falling on the Griffin.

eager and hungry eye. The Griffin did not see this enemy, and soon fell asleep, dreaming, as only an unreal animal can dream, of Crim Tartary and the far-off Baobab tree.   Meanwhile the buzzard slowly narrowed his circles, and at last fell straight on his victim, who rose with a start.   But with savage beak and unpitying talons the greedy bird tore the Griffin limb from limb, for an unreal animal has no bones, and so can offer no resistance.   But its flesh is unreal, too, and so not a mouthful of it could the buzzard swallow.   On the whole this was of great advantage to the Griffin, for when the buzzard, gloating over his prize, tried to devour the flesh, it slipped from his beak just as jelly slips through your fingers.   At last the buzzard fell to the ground completely tired out before he had been able to get a single bite.

Then came the Griffin's turn.   He gathered himself together in haste, for being unreal he had no blood, and therefore could not bleed to death.   In three minutes he was as whole as ever, and before the buzzard had time to rise, the Griffin started off across the fields as fast as legs could carry him.   But he soon became dissatisfied with his progress, and thought that he would try on his wings, which he had not worn for nearly a year.

So he sat down on a log, took his wings from his pocket and shook them out.   They were the Good-year patent gossamer, the very best quality, each of them rolled up in a little case of rubber cloth. He put on the left wing first. After fastening one corner at the shoulder, he slipped his hand through the wristlets, then buttoned it on at the hips, and finally at the knee and the ankle. Lastly he drew his tail through the back loop, and the left wing was all ready for flight.

Then came the right wing. He had fastened it at the shoulder and wrist, but before he could button it on at the ankle, he heard a great rustling noise behind him. In haste he looked around and saw the turkey-buzzard with clenched toes and savage eyes close upon him. The Griffin was scared, as you would surely be to see such a monster after you. He forgot that his wings were not rightly fastened. He forgot everything but the coming of the angry buzzard He spread his wings and away he flew, with the buzzard after him. But he could use only his left wing properly, and so after a little he went around and around in a circle till at last he could fly no longer. He then descended slowly and alighted as best he could upon the dashboard of the doctor's buggy, which stood in front of Absalom Billingslea's store. The terrified horse started to run, tore the stone hitching-post up by the roots, and then off he went, dragging it along, while the Griffin clung to his tail, and the Griffin's wings flapped about him in the wind like a witch's cloak. The horse ran faster and faster, and the hitching-post pounded to the right

Tore the stone hitching-post up by the roots.

and to the left as if it were a great trip-hammer. At last they came to Brushy Creek, where the post struck the bridge with such force as to sink right through with the horse and the Griffin and what there was left of the carriage. The waters of the creek splashed on every side, the sandy bed gave way; in an instant, horse, Griffin, and hitching-post vanished from sight, and the people of Georgia saw them no more.

III.

The Emperor of China was walking one bright morning in the flower garden of the summer palace of the great Wah-Shing. Artificial birds sang in the trees, and the shrubs were made beautiful with gayly colored fans and with little strips of red tinsel paper. The Emperor in that country is a Chinaman, and so all the people that come near him are Chinamen too. It flatters the Emperor to see them look like him. It is for this reason that they become Chinamen. This particular morning he had come out of the Palace Beautiful, clothed in a scarlet robe. His head was freshly shaven, the six long hairs of his mustache were each in its proper place, and in his cue were woven a fresh bunch of red ribbons, for the Emperor wore new ribbons every day. He did this that he might give the old ones to the Lord High Master of the Chamber, whose fees were the old ties of the Emperor's cue.

There is a little pond in the garden of the Emperor's palace, and in this pond is a flock of beautiful white swans. All of them are of the finest porcelain,

which we call "china;" and they are far better than
real swans, because they need no food and never
fly away. The Emperor stopped to admire these
lovely creatures, when all at once the water in the
little lake began to rise. The swans swam apart,
and up through the water rose the head and ears

Up through the water rose the head of a horse.

of a horse. Then came its neck, its forelegs, its
body, and last of all, its tail, and to the very end of
the tail there clung a solitary Griffin. Both horse

and Griffin looked as though they had been on a
long journey. They were smeared with dried mud
and coal dust, and one did not have to look long to
see that both were very much frightened.

He cleared the fence at a bound.

The horse ran furiously across the palace garden.
Coming to the fence around the garden, he cleared it
at a bound, but in doing this the Griffin was caught
between the pickets of the fence and could no longer
keep his hold.

The Emperor with eagerness ordered the Lord
High Master of the Chamber and all his attendants

to catch the horse. They started in pursuit, running as fast as they could. As they ran, their wooden slippers flew off from their feet, but by a skillful kick, such as only a Chinaman can give, each slipper flew high in the air, then forward over its owner's

The Chinamen ran after the horse.

head, falling in front of him, so that without slacking his speed in the least, he could step right into the slipper again.

And thus they ran; the slippers flew over and over their heads, so that it looked as if they were followed by a flock of snow-birds with blue wings, for the slippers of the Emperor's attendants are all white, with blue trimmings. But they never over-took the horse, and for all we know they are running yet, and wherever they are, you may be sure the air is still full of flying slippers.

Meanwhile the Emperor stood alone in the garden, and the poor Griffin lay on the ground beneath the imperial picket fence. His Majesty was very anxious to make the acquaintance of the Griffin, but the lat-ter could not receive the imperial recognition without being formally presented to the Emperor. After much meditation, His Highness bethought himself of a very worthy plan. Possessing all royal authority, he would order himself to bring the Griffin in person to be presented to himself as the Emperor. Thus would the demands of celestial etiquette as well as those of earthly curiosity be satisfied.

And so he walked up to the Griffin, set him on his feet, said to him some assuring words and pre-sented him to the Emperor. The acquaintance thus begun proved to be very pleasant, and the Griffin lived many days in the Emperor's palace. In this time the two became great friends. The Griffin told the Emperor of his many adventures by land and sea, and the Emperor revealed to him the mysteries of

court life, and imparted to him the wisdom of Con-
fucius.   Soon the Griffin was made a mandarin with
the title of Lord High Cousoler to his master, the
Emperor.

All went well until one day when they reclined
together under the shade of a China tree, watching the
gentle movements of the China swans on the little
pond in the garden.   By ill chance the conversation
turned on flying, and the Emperor asked the Lord
High Consoler about his wings and his manner of
using them.   So, to please the Emperor, the Griffin
took them out and put them on ; but while his royal
friend was admiring them, the mischievous Crown
Prince Kin-Sing-Tun came out from behind a camel-
lia bush and tied a bunch of burning cold-chop, or
firecrackers, as we call them, to the Griffin's tail.

It is not strange that the Griffin was startled, for
brave men may well be scared by a thing like that.
He sprang into the air.   His wings spread themselves and bore him away high over the trees.   The
Emperor watched him until he shrank to a little
speck, and the cold-chop on his tail left behind him
a trail of fire.   The Crown Prince had run away in
haste when he found how far his mischief was likely
to go, and the Emperor will not know until he reads

these pages what caused the Lord High Consoler's
sudden flight.

When the Griffin again reached the ground, he
was far away from the palace of the great Wah-
Shing, and even beyond the Chinese wall.   He could

The Griffin flies away with firecrackers on his tail.

not fly back to the Emperor.   He did not know the
way.   And after all he would not be able to make
any. apology which would account for his leaving
without saying good-by.   Besides, the behavior of
the Crown Prince showed him the wickedness of
boys, and made him weary of humanity.   He was

tired of the world, tired of men, tired of living. He
went into the corner of a field and dug a shallow grave in the turf. Then he lay down in the

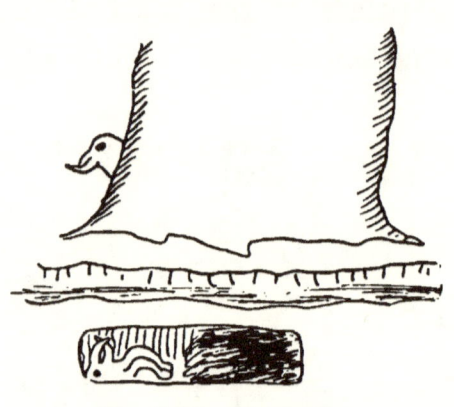

grave, and pulling the
turf over his feet he
rolled up his wings
and closed his eyes.
There he lay for sev-
eral hours trying to
die, but he could not
make it work. Sud-
denly it occurred to
him that, being an

The Griffin tries to die.

unreal animal, he could not die, for only real animals
can die.   When he remembered this he arose with a
sigh, replaced the sods of the grave, and sat down on
them in deep perplexity.

Across the brook on the opposite hill stood a
large tree covered with dense green foliage and fra-
grant with a thousand blossoms. As he looked at
the tree strange memories crowded fast upon him.
Under the tree was great commotion. Little creatures were running hither and thither. Every moment some of them seemed to grow larger and larger,
but as they did so the number became less and less.

At last all was quiet, for there was but one of them left. This one stood quite alone beneath the tree. The Griffin looked at him intently. The old scene came back to him—Crim Tartary, the Baobab tree, and the strange valley of the Quong-Sin-Lee!

He stood for an instant absorbed in his thoughts. "Brother!" he said. They rushed into each other's arms; the two were blended into one, and the problem of the Griffin's life was solved.

They rushed into each other's arms.

ONCE there was a little boy and a little girl, and they lived in a hotel, and they used to like to ride up and down in the elevator. The elevator boy let them do it, because he was a good boy and liked little children. And one day the boy and girl came to the elevator when the elevator boy was gone to lunch, and nobody was there. So they got in and pulled on the rope, and up the elevator went. But they didn't know how to stop it, and so it went on past the third floor, and the fourth floor, and the floor their folks lived on, and they couldn't stop it anywhere. Then it went on up to the top of the hotel, right on up through the roof, and right on up and up, away up into the air, and they didn't know what to do, but just held on and let it go. So it kept going and going and going, and by and by it went clear across to the other side of the earth. And there they were on the island of Formosa, where all the toys are alive, and where the people

166

are just genii, and do nothing at all but witch up things for the children to play with. When they came to the other side and the elevator stopped, it was wrong side up, and they were standing on their heads on the ceiling. But the little boy and little girl didn't mind that, so they turned themselves over and walked out on the ground, and saw all the blue trees with pink leaves and all the funny things that grow in Formosa. Then the little boy picked up a stone and threw it against a blue tree, and as soon as it hit the tree it went "snap!" and all the red leaves on the tree shook and rustled. And up came a genius, and said: "What does the little boy want?" And the little boy said, "I want a popgun." And all at once the popgun came up out of the ground and walked right beside the little boy, so that whenever he wanted to shoot it off all he had to do was to reach out his hand and it was there. And whenever he shot off it went "snap!" and up came a genius, and said: "What does the little boy want?" And it was just the same with the little girl, only she did not care for popguns, but asked for a live parasol which stood all of itself on her shoulder, and every time she shut it up it went "snap!" and up came a genius. And so they had a wonderful time

12

in Formosa, and they played with live ships that steamed about on the gravel walk and sailed over the purple meadow. And you never saw anything in the way of fireworks like their live firecrackers, that would stand up on the rocks and talk to you just before they went off. And the dolls they had and the hobbyhorses, and the live bows and arrows and tin soldiers, every kind of thing that the genii made were as strange as they could be. You wouldn't believe if I should tell you, and I couldn't tell you about half of them if I were to talk all day.

But one morning they got to playing soldier. The little girl closed her parasol and it went "snap!" and the genius came up, and said, "What does the little girl want?" And she asked for ten toy soldiers to stand in a row on the bank and present arms with their toy guns. So the soldiers came up out of the ground and presented arms; for they were all toys, and in Formosa the toys are all alive.

Then the little boy shot off his popgun and it went "snap!" and up came the genius, and the genius said again: "What does the little boy want?" And the little boy asked for ten soldiers big enough to whip the ten soldiers of the little girl. And the little girl's ten soldiers were whipped in the fight they had right there on the banks of the yellow brook. And then the little girl asked for ten more soldiers twice as tall as the others so as to whip her brother's soldiers. Then he had the genius make his twice as tall again so as to whip hers. Then she made hers bigger, and he made his bigger, and they kept the two genii working hard all the time to stretch the soldiers out so as to get each set big enough to whip the others.

Before noon they had got the toy soldiers so big that their heads reached up into the clouds, and when they fought their feet tumbled around and covered almost all of the island of Formosa.

By and by one of the soldiers stepped on the little girl's toe, and she began to cry, and said: "Take me back to mamma!" And the soldier cried too, and his tears came down out of the clouds just like rain.

So the genius told the soldier to stop crying, and then he stretched him out twice as long as ever. Then the soldier reached down and took the little girl in his arms, and he was so tall now that he could reach clear back to the other side of the world. So he put the little girl down softly on the roof of the hotel where her folks lived, and then he stood up and shrank away again until he came back to Formosa.   Then she called "Mamma! Mamma!" and her folks came up on the roof and found her there just as the soldier was slipping back into the clouds, and the people who saw him said it was a cyclone, because they did not know about Formosa and what genii could do.   But the genii forgot to send the elevator back with the little girl, and the hotel man does not yet know what became of it, and he will not know until he reads this story.   So he made a new elevator and put two elevator boys in it so that when one is out to lunch the other will be there, and the elevator will never get away from them.

When the little boy in Formosa found that his sister was gone he did not cry, because he was a boy, and boys know just what to do.   He took his pop-gun and called a genius, "Snap! snap!"

Then he told the genius to get him a berth on the Steamer Nippon Maru for San Francisco.   And when the little boy was ready to start for home he made the genius grow smaller and smaller, so that he could put him into his pocket.   And the genius made himself very small, like a Japanese doll, and the little boy brought him home in his pocket just as he had planned.   But when he got home the little boy could not make him do anything more, for a genius will not go "snap!" when he is away from Formosa.   He is just a little Japanese doll now, and won't do anything at all.   So the little boy keeps him on the shelf with his popguns and bows and arrows and all things, and you will find him lying there to-day, if you go into the house where the little boy's folks live now that they have left the hotel.

But his mother says that the little boy is a genius himself now, and one genius is all she wants in her house.

ONCE there was a little boy who lived in a house with a garden by the side of a great wood. One day the little boy walked out in the garden and saw a spider spinning his web on a rosebush. And the spider had a fat body, covered with brown and yellow hairs, and a yellow head with six little black eyes on the top of it, and eight legs with which he ran up and down on the rosebush. And the spider took a lot of fine thread which he was carrying around in a pocket he had in his body, and out of the thread he made a great web. The web was built of circles of thread, and across the circles he had straight lines of webbing, all meeting at the center just as the spokes meet in the hub of a wheel. And the spider stood at the center with his eight legs spread out and watching with all his eyes. When a fly came against the web it would get tangled in the fine threads, and then the spider would pull up on the web and bring the fly near him. When he could reach the fly, the spider would seize

172

him with his feet and stuff him into his mouth, and so all the meat there was in the fly would become part of the spider.

Then the boy said to himself, "Now I will make me a spider. But my spider shall be big, so that I can catch lions and tigers and bears and all the beasts that live in the great woods." Then the little boy got a great coil of rope and stretched it out from tree to tree in the forest, and part of it he stretched around in circles and part in straight lines from the center out, just like the lines in the web of the real spider. Then he took all the brass kettles and old boilers and sheet iron he could get, and he made out of it all a huge spider. And he covered the body with a buffalo-robe, so that it looked all shaggy with long hairs. And he took a brass kettle for a head, and on it he put six eyes, and every eye was a door-knob. And he made a mouth out of keyholes—twenty of them—one by the side of another. Then out of old stovepipe he made the legs, but he put on nine legs instead of eight, for he wanted to have the best spider in all the woods. And so it was; there was never a spider like it in all the world.

Pretty soon the animals began to come along, the lions roaring and the wolves howling, and they began

to sniff and sniff at the big new spider's web. And
the boy crawled into the spider's body, which he put
in the center of the web, and waited to see what
would happen.

Very soon there was a great scrambling and roaring, and threshing about, and in a minute he saw a
lion fast in the web. And the little boy knew what
to do, for he had watched the spider many a day, and
he did just what he had seen the spider do. He
pulled tight on the web, and slowly drew the lion up
to him. Then he opened the front side of the spider
where his mouth is, and threw the lion down into
one of the front legs. And there it lay just as if it
had been eaten. It was only a mountain lion, and
so not very large; and the legs were big enough to
hold it, for they were as broad as a barrel at the top,
though they grew smaller and smaller toward the toes.

Next a bear comes nosing about, and before he
knew it he too was caught and hauled up and
stowed away in one of the hind legs of the spider.
It was only a cinnamon bear and rather small at that,
so there was plenty of room for him.

Then came an antelope and a woodchuck, and a
catamount, and they were all caught and tucked
away; but in the legs of the spider they all roared

and screamed and showed their white teeth, for they didn't like it a bit. Then he caught a wolf and a coyote and a great horned toad, and stowed them away just as the real spider tucks away the flies. This filled the eight regular legs, and there was just room in the extra one for a wolverene. But when this was caught the little boy himself began to feel crowded. And the coyote nipped his toes, and the catamount scratched his arm, and the horned toad began to stick his horns into him. So the little boy took up the lid of the spider's back, and before he caught any more beasts he crawled out and ran home and never said a word to anybody.

By and by all the people in the little boy's house saw a huge spider bigger than a horse come waddling up the front walk, its thick legs going thumpety-thump as it tumbled along. And they were all scared out of their wits, and ran off in every direction—all but the little boy. He sat on the railing of the veranda and just laughed, for he knew it was only his play spider with an animal in each leg to walk it along. So he laughed again and the animals inside roared and howled and screamed, each one in his own voice; but the lion loudest of all, for the lion is the king of beasts.

Then the hired man got an ax and came up from behind and struck the spider a great blow on the back, which knocked off the lid of the shell.

Then all the animals came out and ran off to the woods, and the spider was empty.

So the little boy crawled into it, and put one arm into one leg and one in another, and one foot in one leg and one in another. Then he walked the spider back to the woods with the other five legs dragging behind. This made it hard work to get along, and he had to see his way by looking out through the six doorknobs.

But when he got the spider back to the woods and was tired of playing with it, the hired man came and took down the web, and they found that there was rope enough in the web for the rigging of sixteen ships. But they were not very large ships.

And now that the little boy is grown up to be a man, he does not play spider any more but tells stories, and this is one of the stories which he told his little boy.

ONCE there was a time when there was a great deal of trouble among the fishes. The big fishes ate the little fishes, and they had to keep running away all the time so as not to be eaten by still bigger ones, and when the little fishes would catch the fishes that were still littler they would eat them too.

And there was so much eating and quarreling and trouble that the fishes made up their minds that they would have a king who would keep them all in order. So they all stood in a row out in the sea one day and agreed among themselves that the one who swam fastest and reached the shore first should be made king of all the fishes. This was because the swiftest fish would be the one that could help the little fishes soonest when some big fish would try to eat them up.

So they all stood in a row and waited for the word to go, and then they swam as fast as ever they

could toward the shore. There was the bass and the
mackerel and the sunfish and the mad tom and the
codfish and the Moorish Idol and all the rest of the
fishes, the little sea horse with the others, each one
swimming with all his might to see if he couldn't
reach the shore before all the others.

By and by one reached the goal ahead of all the
rest, and the other fishes flapped their tails to cheer
him. It was the herring who was swiftest, and so
he was made king.

And the flounder was away behind all the others,
for he swam very slowly with his face close to the
bottom of the sea. So he could not see who had
won the race. When he heard them all flapping
their tails to cheer the king, he called to the sea
horse, who was nearest to him, and asked, "Who is
it they are making king?" And the sea horse called
back, "The herring has won and he is now king of
all the fishes. Three cheers for the herring! he is
all right!" And the others echoed: "Who is all
right? The Herring."

But the flounder was very envious, and twisted
his mouth all on one side, because he wanted to be
king himself. Then he said, "The little naked herring! the little naked herring!" and he looked just

as cross as he could, with his mouth all on one side. When the herring, who was the King of the Fishes, heard what the flounder had said, he issued a ukase that the flounder should wear his mouth on one side after that all the time by way of punishment.

And so the flounder always wears his mouth on one side now, and if you ever catch one you will find it all twisted out of shape, and the only word it can say now is, "The little naked herring!"

But the herring has been king of the fishes ever since, and all the fishes are glad of it, and now there are more herrings in the sea than there are of any other kind of fishes, and you can find one of the king's family anywhere.

THERE once was a lady whose dream
    Was to feed a black cat on whipped cream,
  But the first cat she found
    Spilled the cream on the ground,
And she fed a whipped cat on black cream!

HOW THE SUN BRINGS THE BIRTHDAYS FROM ATKA AND ATTU.

ONCE on a time there were not any children, and there were not any birthdays. So the sun shone all the time, and there wasn't any night and nobody went to sleep. Then all the animals could talk, and wherever you went there they were at it all the time, and you couldn't hear yourself think.

But when the children came they had to have birthdays, and there was such a lot of them that they had birthdays almost every day. Now, there wasn't any one to send off to get the birthday except the Sun, and it took him all night to go and get one, and he could bring but one at a time. For the birthdays are kept away over on the other side of the earth, by the edge of the Icy Sea. And the boys' birthdays they keep piled up on a big rocky island named Atka, and the girls' birthdays are kept on a little mossy island named Attu. And when the Sun goes away over there to get one of the birthdays he is gone all night. Then it is dark, and everybody has to go to sleep till he comes back. It is farther to Attu than it is to Atka, so when the Sun goes after a birthday for a girl he is gone longer than he is when he goes for a boy's birthday. So boys' birthdays seem longer, because the Sun comes back sooner in the morning.

The Sun can only bring one birthday at a time, so orders for birthdays have to be made a long time beforehand or else the children won't have any birthdays at all.

To-morrow morning the Sun will come back from Atka and bring a birthday for Knight, and next week we will send him for Barbara's birthday. She is a little girl, so she has to wait till Knight has had his turn. But the Sun will have to leave to-morrow night again to go to Attu to get a birthday for Elsie Branner or to Atka for Olaf Jenkins or somebody else.

Then to-morrow evening after the Sun is gone the Moon will come along over Mount Hamilton and carry Knight's birthday back to Atka when he gets through with it and has gone to bed. Then the Moon will leave it till Knight wants it again next year. Then the Sun will have to leave California and go back to the Icy Sea to get it. Then it will be night here, because we shall get into the shadow that California makes when the Sun is on the other side of the world.

(*With acknowledgments to John Casper Branner.*)

HIS name was Loro Bonito, for he was a parrot, and Loro Bonito means Pretty Polly in Spanish. He was bright green in color, but his head was yellow, and there was a red epaulet on each of his shoulders. He was born in the woods above the city of Guatemala, but a boy caught him when he was young, and gave him to a little girl who lived in the city, and the little girl's name was Plácida.

And the little girl used to feed him and taught him to speak Spanish. She said to him, " Lorito, quieres tortilla? "—"Little parrot, desirest thou a tartlet? "—for this is the sweet Spanish way of saying, "Polly want a cracker?" And Loro learned to mimic the fife and drum which he heard from the Presidio, where the soldiers were at night and morning. And he learned to call out the numbers of lottery tickets, " Ochociento sessente-ocho," and all the

182

rest of them. And he sang the little Spanish song, "Me gustan todas en general!" which means that all "little girls are nice," as well as some others. But on Sundays little Plácida went to church and heard long sermons in Latin which she didn't understand, so she taught the words to Loro, because she thought he might get some good out of them.

So he learned to say the Latin words after Plácida, and intone them so that every one seemed like the note of an organ—"Peccavi, peccavi, miserere!" he would say, "Per augustá, ad angustá!" and all the rest of it down to "Pax vobiscum!" which some-times came at the end. Then he would change his manner, for so the little girl had taught him, and he would call out in the most cheerful tones, "Vamos á los toros!"—"Let's go to the bullfight!"—for in Guatemala those who go to the church on Sunday morning have a bullfight in the afternoon. People do not do that here in Palo Alto where we live; but it is a warm country, Guatemala is, and that makes a good deal of difference.

One day Loro was missing, and they could not find him anywhere. Little Plácida looked for him high and low, but she could not find him. She called out, "Loro, Loro, quieres tortilla?" and "Pax

13

vobiscum," and "Me gustan todas," but he did not come.

At last her people thought that some cat or calele bird, or some other horrid creature, had carried off Loro, and that he would never be seen again.

And when the water-carrier's boy brought in another parrot whose name was Loro Verde, because he was green, head and all, her father said she might buy him, and she taught him to sing, "Mis ojos negros!" which is easier to learn than "Me gustan todas." It tells all about the black eyes of little girls, for all girls have black eyes in Guatemala.

One day all the people went out to the coffee plantation, which is in the country at Rio Mojara, not far from Guatemala.

And Plácida was sitting on a rock by a brook in the thick shade of the India-rubber tree, humming to herself the song of the black eyes of Manuela, when she heard a strange and wonderful noise in the leaves above her head. It sounded like a great chanting choir, but the voices were high and sharp, and they did not keep in time nor tune. "Peccavi, peccavi!" she heard from the trees, "Miserere Domine." Then it went on, "Per augustá, ad angustá," with the rest down to "Pax vobiscum." Then all were silent for a minute, when a big green parrot with a yellow head flew out from the rest to another tree, laughed a little, and called down to Plácida, "Vamos á los toros!" Then they all flew away with a great rustle, and the little girl never saw them any more. But it seems that Loro Bonito got some good from the sermon, even if Plácida did not.

(*With acknowledgments to A. C. Bassett, Esq., of Menlo Park, Cal.*)

ONCE on a time there was a great tall rabbit, the kind the miners call the "narrow-gauge mule"; but he was not a mule at all, and his real name was "Jack Rabbit." His home was in Montana, and he lived by the river they call the Silver Bow. He could run faster than any of the other beasts, because he could go lickety-clip, lickety-clip over the tops of the sagebrushes, and he did not have any brush of his own to carry.

And there was a Red Fox who lived on the Silver Bow too, and he went hunting because he wanted rabbit meat for dinner. But while he could run very fast, he could not bound over the tops of the sagebrush; for his own brush, which he always carried with him, because he was very proud of it, would catch on the thorns of the other kinds of brush, and so would keep him back.

186

So he sent for his cousin, the Coyote, to come and help him. Now the Coyote lived out in the country by Hardscrabble Mountain, and was not proud at all, for he was big and gray and awkward. He had only a little brush of his own to carry, and no one praised him for his beauty. But with all that the Coyote could run very fast, for he has Indian blood in him. The one trouble was that his hind feet ran faster than his forefeet. So he has to stop every little while and run sidewise awhile to unkink himself and give his forefeet a chance to catch up.

When the Coyote came up they saw the Rabbit bounding along through the bushes, going around in a great circle so that he always came back to the same place. He always liked to do that, for then he could tell just how fast he was getting along.

So the Fox lay low and hid his own brush in the sagebrush, and the Coyote followed the Rabbit around the circle. And he just kept up with the Rabbit all the way, for the Rabbit wasn't scared yet and didn't run very fast. And when they had gone once around the circle the Rabbit passed the Fox, and then the Fox got up and chased him and was only a few feet behind. And the Coyote stopped and ran sidewise for a while to unkink himself, and then he lay down in the bushes and waited for the Rabbit to come back.

The Rabbit was much scared when he saw the Fox close behind him, so he ran and bounded very fast, and the Fox kept falling behind because he had his long brush to carry. But he kept at it just the same, and when the Rabbit came around the circle to where he started there was the Coyote waiting for him. The Rabbit had to make a great jump to get over the Coyote's head. Then they went around again, and the Coyote kept close behind all the way, and the Rabbit began to get tired. When the Coyote's hind legs got tangled up, then the Fox was rested, and he took up the chase. So they kept on, each one tak- ing his turn, ex- cept the Rabbit, who had to take his own turn all the time.

When they came to divide.

Nobody else was there when they came to divide up what they caught; but I saw the Coyote the next day, and he looked so lank and very empty that I think that the Red Fox must

have taken all the rabbit meat for himself.   I think
that he left the Coyote just the ears for his part, and
a rabbit's foot to carry in his pocket for good luck.

THERE once was a faithful old ghost
   Who sat all night long at his post;
At the first break of day
He spanished away
Lest the sun his An-at-omy roast !

WHEN Odin climbed up on his air throne one morning and looked out on the earth, he saw a great big frost-giant away off in the north. The frost-giant walked along until he came to a flock of sheep. Then he seized the shepherd and tossed him out into the water and picked up the sheep and put them into his pocket. Then he lazily walked away over the hills, pulling the sheep out of his pocket and cracking and eating them just as you would eat hazel-nuts.

Odin did not like that sort of thing, so he told his boy Thor to take his hammer and go up there and hammer that frost-giant. So Thor took his hammer and walked over to Jotunheim, where the giants have their castle. When he was outside the castle he found a great hulking fellow who went along with him and carried his baggage, so that Thor hadn't anything to do but to walk around and hit the rocks with his hammer, knocking them all to

190

The frost-giant eating sheep.

pieces, and to tell what he was going to do when he got up among the giants.

They went to sleep that night, and by and by Thor woke up and heard an awful sound like the crashing of all-timbers and the noise of all-thunders. When he heard the noise he was frightened and ran into a house he saw there that was open at one end and had a big room and a little room. He crawled away into the little room and stayed there until the noise stopped. The next time he heard the noise he went out to see what it was, and he found that it was the big boy Scrymir that had come along with him. Scrymir was lying on the ground and snoring away with all his might, and Thor saw that the house he had run into was just Scrymir's mitten that he had thrown off, so big and clumsy that it looked like a house. So Thor took his hammer, for he did not like Scrymir very well, and ran up to him where he was snoring and hit him a big blow in the face with it, striking with all his might. Scrymir stopped his noise for a minute and almost waked up, and he said, " What is this ? Somebody's dropping sand on me ;" and then he went to sleep again and snored again louder than ever, so that the rocks shook and the trees trembled. Then Thor went up to him again, and taking up his big hammer he struck him in the face just as hard as he could, and Scrymir waked up for a moment, and said, " What is this ? I wish these flies wouldn't bother me ;" and then he went to sleep again and snored louder than ever. Then Thor went up to him with his hammer in both hands and struck him just as hard as he could

Thor striking Scrymir with his hammer.

strike, and Scrymir woke up again. " I wish these birds would stop dropping leaves here," he said ; and then Thor ran back into the thumb of the mitten and stayed there till morning.

When it came morning Thor walked up to the gates of the castle of Jotunheim, and the walls of the gate were as high as the sky and he could hardly see to the top of the gate. And when he went in he found the king of the giants, and the king asked him what he wanted. Thor had two men with him, and the king said, "Who are these little fellows that have strayed in here?" And then he asked Thor if there was anything they could do; and Thor said that he

Thor eating against the king's man.

felt so hungry that he could eat an ox. Then the king gave him something to eat, and told him that if he could eat as fast as one of his men, he was a good

deal smarter than he thought he was. So Thor began
to eat with all his might, and ate up the meat just
as fast as he could, but the giant's man ate faster.
Besides, he ate the dishes and all, and the pots in
which the meat was cooked, and Thor looked on
with surprise.

Then the giant reached for his drinking horn, and
said, "Up here we generally drink this at one swallow.
If you are thirsty you ought to do it even quicker
than that." So Thor took up the drinking horn
and drank with all his might; but drink as hard as
he would, he could not empty the horn. It seemed
just as full after he had filled himself with ale as it
was when he began. And the giant looked at him,
and said, "You are a puny fellow if you can not drink
this horn at one swallow." Then he said, "Maybe
you can do something else; maybe you are strong;
there is an old cat on the floor there. Just see if you
can lift her." So Thor went out to the floor, feeling
a little ashamed that he could not empty the drinking horn. Then he took hold of the cat around the
waist, though he could hardly reach around her, and
lifted as much as he could; but strain as hard as he
might, he could not raise one paw. Sometimes he
would move the cat just for a minute, and when he

did that everything seemed to crack. But the cat stuck to the floor, till he gave it up.

And then the king said, "Out there in the yard you will find an old woman. You go out and wrestle with her. She is the weakest one of all of us. Maybe you can throw her. If you can you

Thor trying to lift the cat.

can do more than I think." And so Thor went out and began to wrestle with the old woman, and every time he took hold of her she would trip him up and throw him down on the ground; and he tried again and again. But every time she was too much for him.

So he felt very much ashamed and left the castle and started back on the road from Jotunheim. As he came out of the castle he saw Scrymir coming. Then he looked at him a little closer and saw that Scrymir was the same person as the king of the castle. Then Scrymir, the king of the giants, told Thor how he had been fooled inside the castle; that when he had tried to eat, the man who ate against him was Fire, and Fire could devour the food and the dishes in which the food was kept. The drinking horn he had tried to empty was the ocean itself, and as fast as he drank, so fast the tides would fill it up again. One end seemed like a drinking horn, but the other end was the great sea that never could be dry. Then the cat was no cat at all, but the great Mitgard serpent, whose tail runs around the world and then goes down her own throat, and so holds the whole world together. "When you began to lift on the serpent," he said, "we could hear its bones crack, and we were afraid you might pull it in two, so the earth would all fall to pieces. Then the old woman you wrestled with was Time, and Time goes on forever. Time can throw any man. She will last after you and I and all the giants and all the men on the earth are gone. She can throw us all, and it's no wonder that she threw you."

And then Thor looked at him and saw how his face grew large, and there were great gullies in his cheeks and on his forehead. Then Scrymir said: "Those are the marks of your hammer—great gullies that big trees could grow in, and houses could be built in, and with lairs for wild beasts." And then Thor looked at him again and he saw that Scrymir was no man at all, but the old rough world itself, whose face was covered with the scars of his hammer.

So he went back home to Odin his father and told him that the giants up there in Jotunheim were too big for him to fight with. If he went there again he must have a new hammer, and it must be as large as all the earth.

ONCE there was a lot of boys, and they lived in the edge of the great fir forest by the side of the Icy Sea. So they played leapfrog and jumped over each other's head just as frogs do. And one day, when they were having great fun and were going over one another's heads in fine shape, Perseus came flying along, carrying the head of Medusa. And Perseus stopped to look at the boys, and before he thought what he was doing he had turned the old head toward them and changed them all into stone.

And there the boys were. They couldn't get down and they couldn't come apart, for they were all stone together. And Perseus saw their father coming, so he flew away as fast as he could, for he knew that their father wouldn't like it when he saw what he had done with the old head of Medusa.

When the father saw the boys one above another and all fastened tight and turned into stone. he felt very bad and began to cry. But that didn't do

14   199

any good, so he took the boys home and set them up in front of his house.

And there they are yet, and when you go up to the Icy Sea and stop at the little village of Ka-Ke, where the Haida people live, by the edge of the fir woods,

The boys that played leapfrog.

there you will see the boys that played leapfrog, set up right in front of the house. And there are a lot of other funny things there too, and if you don't know what they all are, the thing to do is to go right into the house and ask about them.

IT was the King of the Weirds, and he sat in a tower of his castle. And all around him on the walls the Weirds stood and wept, and on the tallest turret the black crow sat and said, "Caw, caw, caw!" And the castle stood by the shore of the sea, and the King looked far over the waves to the Monkeys' Island. And the Prince of the Weirds, the King's little boy, lay in his trundle-bed by the throne and moaned all the time. And the Prince was very sick, for he had eaten the green fruit from the jujube tree, and there was nothing could save him but a monkey's liver. And the Weirds all wept as they stood on the walls of the castle, and the black crow on the turret said "Caw, caw!" And the Prince could not play with his live toy soldiers, or his golden popgun, or his sugar dog Tiny, but lay in his bed and moaned and cried for monkey's liver.

So the King pounded on the floor with his scepter and called "*What ho!*" Then he sent to the

* After a Japanese tale, translated by Mr. A. H. Chamberlain.

shore for his favorite Jellyfish, who ran on errands for him in the sea just as the black crow ran on errands in the air. The Jellyfish came up from the water and touched his hat to the King, and said: "What does your Majesty command?" Now in these days the Jellyfish was a sure-enough fish. And it had head and tail and fins enough to swim with, and a place where it could fold them up when it wanted to walk out on the beach. For the Jellyfish had legs, too, and could walk, and he wore a hat and carried a sword by his side, and he looked like a little soldier when he stood on shore. And the Prince liked to play with the Jellyfish, and they dug holes in the sand together and made sand pies and sometimes they went wading in the surf.

So the Jellyfish came walking up the stairs with his sword by his side and his fins nicely folded in the sheath down his back. And the King said, "What ho! You must swim away across the sea to the Monkeys' Island, and bring me a monkey with his liver in."

And the Jellyfish touched his hat, and shook out his fins and ran down the stairs to the sea and swam away and away, just as the King had told him. And the Weirds all watched him while he swam, and the tears ran down their faces, and the black crow on the turret said, " Caw, caw ! "

When the Jellyfish came to the Monkeys' Island, · he saw a Monkey sitting on the limb of a tree.   And

He saw a Monkey sitting on the limb of a tree.

the Monkey looked pleased, for he had never seen a Jellyfish before, and he was very tired of living with the monkey people and seeing nobody but monkeys, monkeys, monkeys everywhere, just like a great menagerie. So the Jellyfish said, "Come, Monkey, don't you want to go out for a sail on the water? Come to the land of the Weirds with me and I will show you the King and the Castle and the little Prince of the Weirds, and the crow that says 'Caw' on the turret."

"All right," said the Monkey, and he climbed down the tree in two jumps, and took the Jellyfish by the hand, for Jellyfishes had arms and hands in those days as well as legs and fins and bones and everything.

And the Jellyfish told the Monkey to get on his back. Then he spread his fins and leaped into the sea. Away they went, over the waves till they came to the shore by the King's castle. And all the Weirds stood up and looked at them, and the crow said, "Caw, caw! Beware, O Monkey, with your liver in." So the Jellyfish shook off the salt water, and dusted the sand from his feet and folded his wet fins. Then he took the Monkey by the arm, and arm in arm they went up the marble stairs to the throne of the King of the Weirds. "What ho!" said the King, "and have you brought me the Monkey with the liver in?"

Then he called to the chief cook to come in and

carve the Monkey, and the cook came in and sharp-
ened his knife on a stone.

Then the Monkey was scared, and he ran up the
wall and sat on the top of the throne chattering
away to himself and shivering as if he were cold.

And the King could not understand him, and
said, "What ho, O Monkey! what is this you say?"

And the Monkey got his voice again, for in those
days all the animals could talk. That was before
there were so many little children to do the talking
for all. And the Monkey said, "I am so sorry, O
great King. My liver is so heavy that I always
leave it at home when I go visiting. It is over on
the Monkeys' Island hanging on the limb of the tree
where I have my home. Oh, if you had only told
me, then I would have brought it along, and his
highness the Prince would have been well again."
Then the Monkey said, "Wo is me!" and the
Weirds all wept and the crow said "Caw, caw!"

And the King said, "What ho, O Jellyfish! take
the Monkey home and bring his liver only back
with you."

So away they swam again to the Monkeys' Island,
and the Monkey clung tight to the Jellyfish and
shivered as he chattered to himself in a language the

Jellyfish could not understand. When they came to the shore the Monkey ran swiftly up the tree and climbed on the long branch. "Wo is me!" he called to the Jellyfish, "I am undone and all is lost. My liver is gone. Some one has stolen it. And what will the poor Prince do?" Then he chattered away to himself, and softly opened and closed one eye to let a tear fall from it, and it dropped down on the nose of the Jellyfish.

And the Monkey chattered again, and all the other monkeys heard him and ran away, and each one took his liver with him, so the Jellyfish could not find a liver anywhere.

In the Castle of the Weirds the King sat and gnashed his teeth, and said: "What ho!" when he saw the Jellyfish swimming back alone. And the Weirds all wept again, and the sick Prince groaned and the black crow said "Caw, caw! beware of the Monkey, O King, beware!"

When the Jellyfish came up from the beach and entered the castle gate the King went out to meet him. He threw down his scepter as he stepped off the throne. He picked up his umbrella which was standing in the hall, and he pounded the Jellyfish with it until he broke every bone in his body. Then he beat him again till he hadn't any fins or any bones, or any tail, or any legs, or anything else in him but just jelly.

Ever since then all the Jellyfishes there are in all the seas have been just as he was when the King had finished with him. They all swim about in the water without a bone in their body, without any fins or any tail, or any legs. Because their legs are all pounded to jelly they never walk out on the land, but swim around in the sea. And they open and shut themselves just like an umbrella, because it was an umbrella that the King took when he beat the first Jellyfish all to fine jelly and made a sure-enough Jellyfish out of him.

W E called him Bob. We never knew his real
name. That had been left in the jungles of
Borneo. He was born in 1890, a prince of the tribe
of *Cercopithecus* which inhabits the palm forests of
the South Sea Islands. Stolen from his parents by a
South Sea trader, he was brought to San Francisco,
exchanged for a keg of beer, and found his way at
last to a Kearny Street curiosity shop.

Not long after, a student of evolution saw him
there, ransomed him by a subscription from his fel-
low-students, and Bob was transferred to a new home
in the university beside the Tall Tree. Here he was
placed in the custody of a young naturalist from
Japan. Otaki being likewise Asiatic by birth, understood the wants and feelings of Bob better than
did any of the others by whom he was surrounded.

We first knew Bob as a wild and suspicious creature, who looked at all who came near him with fear
or hatred. If any person touched him, Bob would

look him straight in the eyes, with scowling face and
lips rolled back, every muscle tense for action in case
of any injury or indignity. Whenever he was lifted
from the ground, all these expressions would be in-
tensified; but he never ventured to bite any one who
seemed beyond his size, or to escape from any one he
thought able to hold him. Toward women he showed
from the first great aversion, for they had poked him
in the ribs with their parasols while he was in prison
in Kearny Street. Furthermore, he seemed seriously
to disapprove the starnge freedom allowed to women
in our country. In such matters, our manners and
customs are very different from those which prevail
in the tribe of *Cercopithecus* in Borneo.

After a time, under protest, he let one young
woman lead him about by his chain, and refrained
from open enmity; but he never gave her either trust
or affection. Children he held in utter abhorrence,
for it was their delight to ridicule him and to vex his
dignity with sticks and clods of earth. When any of
them came near him he would jump at them, hissing
and scolding, and often only the strength of his chain
saved them from injury.

When Bob came from Kearny Street his hair was
infested with the small, louselike parasite (*Hæmato-*

pina quadrumanus) which always abounds where
those of his race are gathered together. Bob did not
try to conceal this fact; he made it the joy of his lei-
sure. A large part of his time was spent in searching
his arms and legs in quest of the insect. When he
found or pretended to find one, he would eat it with
much appearance of satisfaction, keeping up all the
while a vigorous smacking of the lips. A young
entomologist became interested in this, and sought to
make for himself a collection of these insects from
Bob's hair. But while he made his explorations,
putting his captures in a small vial, Bob conducted
a similar search among the hairs on his friend's hand.
The bystanders laughed heartily, but Bob saw nothing funny about the affair. If one could judge by
his movements and the smacking of his lips, he was
more successful than the naturalist himself. But all
this with Bob was simply an excess of politeness.
In his tribe of *Cercopithecus* it is the height of courtesy for one individual to go over the head and shoulders of his friends, taking hold of hair after hair,
drawing them through his fingers, so that no parasite
can escape. If a stranger in any way earns his good
will, Bob will show it by devoting himself to this
search either on hand or coat sleeve. At these times

Bob is the perfection of courtesy. He pretends to find numberless *Hæmatopinæ* on his friend's hands, even though you can see with your own eyes that he finds nothing at all. And all the time he chuckles and smacks his lips as though each discovery were an object of personal satisfaction to him.

Of snakes, large or small, Bob has always stood in abject terror. If he is held firmly and the snake is placed near him, he looks piteously in the face of his keeper; and sometimes, more in sorrow than in anger, he will bite if he is not let go. At one time a snake in a paper bag was shown him. When the paper bag was afterward left near him, he would furtively approach and open it, to peep a moment shiveringly into its depths, and then retreat ignominiously, only to approach for another peep when he had summoned sufficient courage.

A live salamander was placed on the table by his side. This he looked at with a great deal of interest, finally taking it in his hands, with many precautions. When he saw how inert it was, he laid it down and lost all interest in it.

Toward a flat skin of a coyote and one of a wild-cat, used as parlor rugs, Bob showed the same fear as in the presence of the snake. If one brought them near him he would jump wildly about or cower in terror behind a chair. This instinctive fear is apparently an inheritance from the experience of his fathers, whose kingdom was in the land where tigers and snakes were dominant and dangerous. A similar skin without hair and eyes he cared nothing for. At one time he climbed on the back of a chair to get away from the coyote skin. The chair was overturned by his efforts. He saw at once that when the chair fell it would carry him backward to the coyote, so he let go of the chair and, seizing his chain, swung himself off out of the reach of the coyote, while the chair was allowed to go over. This was repeated afterward with the same result.

Bob grew very expert in the use of this chain, which he came at last to regard as a necessary part of his environment. In climbing chairs or trees he always took it into consideration. He never learned to untie knots in it, but would very deftly straighten it whenever it became tangled or kinked. Sometimes he would break fastenings, escaping to the top of the house, clanking his chain as he went. It was not easy to catch him then, for he delighted in freedom. At such times he would manage the chain most skillfully, going back to set it free if it caught

on any projection. When very hungry, however, he
would come down to the ground or sit patiently outside the kitchen window, waiting to be coaxed and
caught. At one time after we had been entreating
him for an hour, he came down from the house in a
rage to scare away some boys who were mocking him
from below, and who fled in terror at his approach.
When loose in the tall grass, Bob would walk on his
hinder limbs, holding his head high, and looking
about for birds, in whom he seemed to take much
interest. For some reason their calls attracted him.
His hands meanwhile were held with drooping wrists
like the wrists of persons afflicted with the Grecian
bend. Toward most animals and toward persons he
could not frighten he usually affected perfect indif-
ference, often not deigning to grant them even a
glance.

Toward horses and cows, and to other animals
"big and unpleasant" to him, he held a great dislike.
When Willy, the saddle horse, came near him, Bob
would crouch like an angry cat, erecting his hair,
humping his back, and scolding vehemently. When
in his judgment he was safely out of Willy's reach,
he would advance boldly and scold loudly. When
he thought Willy too near, he became as small and

inconspicuous as possible, to avoid the horse's notice. At one time he was placed on Willy's back, where he went into spasms of fear. When taken into the house, he grew bolder, and, climbing on the back of a chair, he described his adventures volubly and with many gestures to his friend Otaki, who understood it all.

To the big dog Rover he also had strong objections. Rover looked down on Bob with tolerant contempt, as a disagreeable being, not to be shaken like a rat because possibly human. But when Bob would strike him in the face with the flat of his hand, Rover would snap at him, barking indignantly; but he never caught him, and Bob was careful to keep out of his reach. His discretion could be counted on to get the better of his courage. With the little terrier, Dandy, Bob's relations were often friendly, although there was very little mutual trust. At one time Dandy was deep in the ivy in search of a rat, while Bob had also entered the ivy by another opening for other reasons. They met in the dark in a rat-hole through the ivy leaves, and a sharp conflict ensued, marked by much scolding on the one part and pulling of hair and barking on the other. When Dandy had dragged Bob to the light, both were very

much surprised, and they parted with mutual apolo-
gies and much shamefacedness.

One day a big saucy blue-jay saw Bob, and, after
the fashion of his kind, fluttered up to him and
showed his contempt by screaming "Ja-a-ay!" under
Bob's nose. Bob reached out one hand softly,
caught the bird by his tail, and then pulled out, one
by one, all his gay feathers. When the bird was
naked Bob went to work and soberly ate him, and
the other blue-jays never screamed "Ja-a-ay" at him
after that.

Being offered a glass of milk, Bob looked at it
for a moment, then took the glass in both hands and
drank from it. His mouth being small, much of the
milk was spilled on the floor. Being then offered a
glass partly full, he handled it more deftly, seeming
to understand how to use it. When offered a pewter
cup with a handle, he took it in both hands and
drank as from the glass, but, noticing the handle, he
set the cup down and raised it again properly. Then
he drank from it as a child of any other race would
have done. He soon learned to drink water from
bottles. If the bottle were large, he would use one
of his hands to hold it, guiding it to his mouth by his
hinder legs. At the first trial he understood the
15

purpose of the cork, which he would draw with his teeth. Then he would look down into the neck of the bottle to see if the water were really there and

Indulgence.

no deception practiced on him. He also usually shook the bottle before drinking, apparently a custom in Borneo. Once a bottle of carbonated mineral water ("Napa soda") was given him. He drew the cork, much surprised at the explosion, and the character of the water caused him equal surprise; still he drained the bottle and was apparently pleased with it. A bottle of claret being offered him, he drank eagerly and became much exhilarated, but at the same time much confused. After this he always declined claret, putting the bottle away with a gesture of disapproval. Of water colored by fruit juices he was very fond.

Being left alone in a student's room, he experimented on the bottles there. He drew the cork from bottles of ink and of bay rum; not relishing the contents of either, he poured both into the wash basin.

When he was offered an empty egg-shell, he raised it up and looked into the crack from which the contents had been taken. Then he would use his fingers to pull the shell apart, licking the inside, but apparently disgusted with the small amount of food it contained.

Being shown his reflection in the mirror, he advanced toward it scowling, but soon detecting the sham, he lost all interest in it. A hand glass was given him, but he paid very little attention to his reflec-

Repentance.

tion in it, laying it down and turning to other things.

At one time a brood of chickens became motherless because a coyote from the mountains had invaded their home. One little white chicken came into Bob's hutch and Bob treated it with great

Resolution.

kindness. As the chicken grew larger, it always left the roost at night and curled itself up on the blanket in Bob's arms. When he fed in the morning, if the chicken were in his way or ventured to touch his food, he would take it in both hands and lay it softly to one side with the greatest seriousness of demeanor.

The life of Bob was not without its tender passages. He was loved in turn by the vivacious Mimi and the gentle Nanette. The two stood in much the same relation as the

" . . . ladies twain
Who loved so well the tough old dean."

In Borneo, among the tribes of *Cercopithecus*, the

male is easily the lord of creation. The female ex-
pects to be crowded aside and frequently punished,
and takes rude treatment as a matter of course. A
kind expression now and then, an occasional hour
devoted to hunting *Hæmatopinæ* in her hair, or even
a cessation of blows and bites, and she is thankful
and satisfied.

Mimi was of the tribe of *Macacus*, gentle in manner, excessively quick of foot, impatient of restraint
or even touch from any hand except that of her
chosen lord and master. She had large, projecting
gray eyes—"pop-eyes" her rivals might have called
them—and a wrinkled face suggestive of an age she
did not possess. Her face readily assumed an expression of most impatient contempt if any one not
of her race attempted to caress her or to take any lib-
erty with her. Mimi had been brought as a child
from the South Sea Islands, and had grown up in a
Mayfield beer-hall, where she had learned to drink
beer with the rest of them, and in general "knew the
world," as most of us who live outside the jungles of
Borneo are compelled to know it.

Mimi pleased Bob from the first, though he was
careful never to let her forget her proper station. If,
for example, she had any food he wanted, or if others

showed her special attention, he would seize her chain, draw her up to him, and bite her forcibly in the neck, which is the time-honored sign of domestic supremacy in Borneo. At this she would squeal lustily, but she never offered resistance or showed any kind of resentment. Masculine supremacy is acknowledged in the tribe of *Macacus* as in that of *Cercopithecus*. Often Bob would draw Mimi to him to bite her in the neck, apparently to remind her of his superiority. At night they slept together in the hutch, each with a soft arm round the other's waist.

Nanette, who came later, was also of the tribe of *Macacus*, but she was of a different branch of the great family. She was much larger than Mimi, nearly as large as Bob himself. She had lived in a French family, where she had acquired her name and her calm, considerate manner. She was a gentle blonde, with a pensive, averted face, as though the present was merely an object of toleration with her. Evidently Nanette had had a history, but what that history was no one now can tell. Perhaps there was no history, and her sadly patient expression came from the absence of one.

Mimi was soon very jealous of Nanette, but without good reason; for Bob treated Nanette with uniform contempt, pushing her about and biting her in the neck whenever she came near him. In this Mimi would assist, often seizing Nanette's chain and pulling her about till she was brought within Bob's reach. After a time Mimi's former master returned; she went back to her drinking of beer, grimacing at visitors, and Bob and this history sees her no more.

Meanwhile Nanette and Bob were left together. He remained contemptuous toward her, robbing her of her food and treating her with indignity. Often, when others were looking, Bob would show his authority over her by ostentatiously drawing up her chain and nipping her in the neck; but at other times, when no one was watching, he would relax his dignity and the two would lie for hours in the sunshine, each picking fleas from the other's hair. However roughly she was treated, Nanette never showed resentment, and seemed only too glad to be the slave of her royal Bob.

At one time Bob had treated Nanette with peculiar severity, for which reason Lady Erica gave him a good beating. Nanette, the gentle, took his part, turned on the lady, and would have severely bitten her had she not been taken off. For two months after, whenever Lady Erica approached Nanette, she would fly into a passion, scolding, trying to bite, and showing every sign of hate possible to the race of *Macacus.* But Bob had only contempt for feminine wrath and its manifestations. Whenever Nanette made any demonstration against the lady, Bob would seize her and bite her in the neck until she cried for pain. But all this time she would not look at him, but kept her wrathful eyes fixed on the lady, willing to suffer anything rather than have Bob's feelings hurt.

Nanette would often leap into the lap of her keeper, seeking the caresses she did not always secure from Bob. This she would do with the manner of a lapdog or a pampered cat. But Bob never sought caresses. He was always earnest, never in the least playful or sentimental. Any new proposition he always took seriously. He expected the worst, and scowled and showed his teeth until the matter was thoroughly understood, when he usually became indifferent.

One day the children vexed him overmuch, and breaking his chain he came out among them. They fled in consternation, all but the younger one, who was a brave little Knight, and who stood his ground, though at the cost of a serious biting.

And thus it came that after two years of freedom Bob returned to the curiosity shop in Kearny Street—not the one on the right as you go up Pine Street, but the other one, where the red-tailed parrots scold and swear, and among whose oaths you may hear all the varied languages of the South Sea Islands. And there in a little iron cage he remains cramped and unhappy. All day long he rolls back his sneering lips, shakes the cage by pulling against the bars, and swings himself to and fro, trying to overturn the cage and cast it on the floor. And here he waits till his ransom is paid again. Fifteen dollars, I believe, is the sum at which it is fixed. Whoever does this will open for him the door for another series of adventures.

And in fact, I found to-day that some one has already done this ; for passing the door of the "Midway Plaisance," a dime museum on Market Street, I heard a familiar call. It was Bob. He was sitting on a divan with a muscle-dancer from Cairo, joyously scowling and surveying with grim complacency the sordid attractions of the dime museum. They all belonged to him, and he was happy, for he would have had nothing more glorious had he inherited all the treasures of the Borneo kingdom of all his ancestors.

A FTER Bob had left us, there wasn't any monkey at all about the house for a month. Then Algernon Fitzclarence Macpherson came down from the city of San Francisco. He had come over from Southern China in search of adventures, and had got as far as California. His real name was Macacus, but Macpherson sounds better and fits better with the rest of his name.

He had a red nose and brown whiskers, but the hair on the top of his head was black, and he wore it pompadour. He was a very dignified monkey person, and would allow no familiarities, but at the same time he liked to understand whatever was going on.

One day when the sun was very hot we tied him to a tree, and then set the garden sprinkler to work by his side. It went whizzing round and round, throwing cold drops of water all over Fitzclarence and making him feel very ticklish. At last he climbed upon it to see what made it act so, and then

he went round and round with the sprinkler. Then
he climbed down again, because he saw that this
would not do. Then he got back away as far as he
could and ran against the sprinkler with all his
might and pushed it over. Then it could not whirl
round and round any more, and he felt very proud
because he had conquered the sprinkler. And after
that he knew just what to do every time when the
sprinkler was set going near him. But he never
learned how to turn the water off and on.

In those days a big blue dog lived at the Jazmin
House. He was the kind of dog they called. the
Great Blue Dane, and so we named him Hamlet, for
some one said that Hamlet was a blue Dane too. He
lived in the barn and had rooms just below the
apartments of Fitzclarence, and the two were great
friends. Fitzclarence liked to ride on Hamlet's back,
and sometimes he would bite Hamlet's ear just to
hear the great dog growl. And when Fitzclarence
would catch a chicken and pull its feathers all out,
Hamlet would laugh till his sides would shake.

Sometimes we used to let Hamlet take care of
Fitzclarence, and we did this by tying Fitzclarence's
chain into Hamlet's collar so that the two could go
off together to play whenever they would. The

chain would make sure that Hamlet would bring Fitzclarence back all right.

But whenever the carriage went out over the hills Hamlet liked to go along. One day it chanced that he and Fitzclarence were at play together, and did not notice that the horses were harnessed to the carriage. And when he saw us driving away, Hamlet forgot all about his charge and everything else, and dashed off through the garden, among the trees, and then down the road after the carriage.

And Fitzclarence came after him because he had to. First he stood on his legs and tried to run with the dog. Then he struck into a rosebush and went through it without stopping for the thorns. Then he struck an oak tree and saw all sorts of stars. Then he came into the road and his hair was full of dust. Then he reached a little pond of water, and he was dragged through it like a wet rat. And when they overtook the carriage he had gone half a mile. But some one who saw him coming stopped Hamlet and untied Fitzclarence and fastened him to a tree.

Then Hamlet ran away, because he was ashamed of what he had done to Fitzclarence. It was hard to tell whether he was a monkey or a mop.

And when I came up to him, Fitzclarence looked at me very reproachfully, as much as to say: "How dare you be so careless!"

Then I put Fitzclarence on the seat of the bicycle, and wheeled him home all the way. He was as stern as the king of Spain, and I felt as humble beside him as if I had been dragged through the mud by a blue Dane ogre myself.

And after that Fitzclarence would never be tied to Hamlet; and he would never joke nor play with me, but fell back on that lofty dignity which is so becoming to owls and monkeys, but which other people do not know how to put on.

O LD Sea Catch was at home when the pirate ship came to Zapalata. So he sat on the rocks where he lived, and roared and groaned. For Zapalata is on Medni Island, far to the Northwest in the edge of the Icy Sea. And it is very cold at Medni, and the green waves are like ice. So old Sea Catch wore his sealskin overcoat all summer long, and all winter too. And Matka, his wife, had a sealskin sacque on, and little Kotik wore a small sealskin jacket, too, and it was black, just like his father's overcoat. But Matka's sealskin sacque was gray and brown.

And because Sea Catch and all his family wore sealskin sacques, the pirate ships used to come up to Medni to steal their clothes away from them. There was so much fog and storm, for Medni is one of the Storm King's own islands, that the pirates could come and go as they pleased. People could not keep them away even though the cruiser Yakut followed after them night and day, and the watchman on the cliffs slept with his hand on his rifle. And the pirates used to trouble old Sea Catch a great deal too, and kept him roaring and groaning all the time, while the tears ran down his cheeks.

One night when the fog was very thick so that old Sea Catch could hardly see how to roar, and little Kotik couldn't find his way down to the beach, one

Sea Catch.

of the pirate schooners sailed out of the darkness and cast its anchor in the sea close to Zapalata. And old Sea Catch roared with all his might when he saw the captain coming on shore in his canoe. The schooner was called Red Light, but that was not her real name, because she was a pirate schooner. Pirates don't have any real name, and the captain did not have any name either—just Pirate.

So Captain Pirate came up to Sea Catch and asked him for his sealskin overcoat, and Matka's sealskin sacque and little Kotik's black jacket.

Then Sea Catch shook his head very quickly and roared, which meant that he couldn't have anything.

The Red Light.

Then the captain of the Red Light saw all the bachelor folks sleeping out on the rocks, each one with a nice clean sealskin coat, which kept him warm and kept the rocks from hurting him. Then he asked old Sea Catch if these bachelors belonged to his family, and Sea Catch shook his head and growled, which meant that they did not. Then the captain

asked Sea Catch if the bachelors needed sealskin
coats any longer, and Sea Catch shook his head three
times and growled very loudly, which meant that he
didn't care.

So Captain Pirate, with his men, went out on the
rocks and took all the sealskin coats away from the
bachelors. Then they put them into the canoe and
went back to the Red Light which was waiting for
them in the mist, and there were a thousand of them
in all, all sealskin coats and jackets, and they rolled
each one up in salt and tied them with a string;
then they packed them in a big drygoods box, which
stood on the deck just behind the mainmast.

And when they left the shore, old Sea Catch
roared again very loudly, and little Kotik growled as
well as he could so as to scare the pirates away.

And while they were roaring, all of a sudden the
great fog broke, and the sun who hadn't been at
Medni for six weeks, looked right in on them to see
what was going on.

And right around Palata Point the steamer Yakut
was sailing straight toward the Red Light.

So the pirate captain hoisted his sails as quietly as
he could and started away. And on the top of the
mainmast he swung out the flag of a Russian mer-

16

chantman, with its bands of white and blue and red, so that the Yakut would think he was not a pirate, and would let him sail away to his home at San Francisco.

But the Yakut was too smart for that, and the big steamer put out her flag of white with a blue cross, which showed that she was a Russian man-of-war.   Then she bore down on the Red Light, and it didn't take long for the Yakut to catch her.

And old Sea Catch sat on the rocks and roared and groaned three times for the captain of the Red Light.   And then he shook his head, which meant that it was wrong to be a pirate and to steal sealskin coats.

So the Red Light had to come to a stop and took down her flag of white, blue, and red, which didn't belong to her at all.

Then the captain of the Yakut went on board the Red Light and found the box full of sealskin coats, each one rolled in salt and tied up with a string.

So he took them all and put them in big canvas bags, and tied them up with a rock in the bottom of each bag.   Then he sunk them all in the sea.   And there they are all now at the bottom of the Icy Sea, just off the southern end of Medni Island.   But if

you go there you won't find them, because the water
is deep and green and cold, and there is so much fog
you won't know the place when you see it.

Then the captain of the Yakut fastened a long
rope to the Red Light's nose and hitched her on behind, and then they started for the nearest town,
which is away across the sea of Okhotsk, and its name
is Vladivostok.

And when they got to Vladivostok the Yakut
would have hauled the Red Light up on the bank
and have left her there for the winds and the waves
to batter to pieces, just as the Rush hauled out the
Onward and the Thornton, the Carolina and the
Angel Dolly on the Unalaska sands the week before.

But when the Yakut was sailing away dragging
the Red Light behind her, all at once a great storm
came up. And the fog was so thick that you could
cut it with a knife, and so dark that after you had
cut it you couldn't have found the place.

Then Captain Pirate took out an ax and chopped
the long rope which held his boat to the Yakut.
Then he put up all the sails he had, and the Red
Light went right off the other way. And it was so
dark that the Yakut could not find the Red Light
anywhere.

Then the Red Light started for Yokohama, which is the name of the queer old Japanese city where the children's toys are all alive. And when she had sailed two days the fog lifted and the Yakut caught sight of her in the distance. And the big steamer ran very fast, with the white flag and the blue cross waving on her topmast. But the Red Light put out the British Union Jack, all blue with the crosses of white and red. Then she sailed as fast as she could, though this was not her own real flag either.

Then the Yakut fired a gun at her, but did not hit her, and just as she was going to fire again the Red Light came into the harbor of Yokohama.

And there lay at anchor a great British man-of-war, and her name was Sea Dog, and the little Red Light slipped in behind her and put down her flag and her sails.

And when the Yakut came around the headland into the harbor, all she saw was the great ship Sea Dog with the Union-Jack flag on every mast and her big guns looking straight at the Yakut.

So the Yakut saluted with her blue-cross flag, which meant "Good morning," just as if nothing had happened. Then the captain of the Sea Dog fired a gun, which meant "How do you do?" And then the

Yakut waved her flag again, which meant "Good-by." Then the Red Light slipped out from behind the great ship Sea Dog, and the captain sailed to Yokohama city, where he went ashore and bought some Japanese candy and some firecrackers.

And all this time old Sea Catch sat on his rocks at Zapalata, and roared because the pirate stole the bachelors' sealskin coats and lost them in the sea. And if you ever go through the Storm King's gate into the Icy Sea, inquire the way to Zapalata, and you will see old Sea Catch sitting there yet.

Then he will roar and shake his head, which means that this is a true story, and the tears will roll down his cheeks; and this is a warning to all pirates. But when you hear the Yakut whistle you need not be afraid, if you have not stolen any sealskin sacques.

The Red Light.

"Let me alone," said Kotik.

THE BABY SEAL.

"O MATKA," said I, "may I look at your baby seal?" "Yes, you may," she said, "but I must go and wash my face." Then Kotik, the baby seal, said: "I do not like you; you go away and let me alone. If you do not go I will bite you, and I will tell Atagh, my father, and he will snort at you and bite you, too. Let me alone," said Kotik.

So Matka went off to wash her face in the sea. But Atagh did not like to have her go, and he groaned over the troubles of married life so that one could hear him a mile away. And he leaned back in his seat when he groaned, and opened his mouth wide, and threw his head back and groaned again.

But Matka tried to get past him to go to wash her face. And Atagh said, "Matka, you shall not go." So he seized her by the neck and flung her over his shoulder back into her place. "See me," he said, "I never wash my face. I have stayed right here at home two whole months hard at work, and I have never once indulged in frivolity." Then Atagh saw me, and he groaned again. "Go away," he said. "Don't you see how hard it is to manage a family, and visitors make it all the harder." And Kotik groaned too in his little, high-pitched voice: "Don't you see how hard it is to have you standing around? It is all that we can do to manage Matka, anyhow."

Then Polosikatch, Matka's brother, who was sitting alone on a rock, began to laugh. But Atagh snorted at him, and he ran away as fast as his pudgy feet could carry him, and on his way he tumbled over little Holustiak, and they both bumped their noses against the rock and had to run down to the sea to wash their faces.

And Matka, who waited her time, sat quite still and craned her neck, looking at me all the while with sleepy, curious eyes.

"Do go away," said Atagh. "Don't you see what heavy responsibilities I have?" Then he began to pant; for he was stout and scant of breath, and he groaned again when he thought of all the responsibilities of life.

And Kotik climbed on a stone and began to cry. But no one took any notice of him, so he wiped

Matka.

his eyes with his flat, brown hands and went off to play with the Sivutch's little boys. But the Sivutch babies would not play with him. "We are big," they said, "but we don't know anything. Go off and play with some one else. We are going to learn to swim to-morrow." And they opened their mouths very wide and cried as loud as they could. And Kotik saw a pod of little black seal pups, just like himself, crawling up a flat rock and sliding back every time they got half way up.

Then he went up to climb and slide, and for all I know he is climbing and sliding yet.

ONCE there was a little blue fox and his name was Eichkao, and he was a thief. So he built his house down deep among the rocks under the moss on the Mist Island, and his little fox children used to stay down among the rocks. There they would

The little blue thief.

gurgle, gurgle, gurgle, whenever they heard anybody walking over their heads. Eichkao and his fox wife used to run all around over the rocks to find something for them to eat, and whenever he saw anybody

239

coming he would go clin-n-n-g, cling-g-g, and his voice was high and sharp, just like the voice of a buzz saw.

One day he walked out on the rocks over the water and began to talk to the black sea-parrot, whose name is Epatka, and who sits erect on a lazily built nest with one egg in it, and wears a great big bill made of red sealing wax. He has a long, white quill pen stuck over each ear, and over his face is a white mask, so that nobody can know what kind of a face he has, and all you can see behind the mask is a pair of little, foolish, twinkling, white, glass eyes. What the two said to each other I don't know, but they did not talk very long; for in a few minutes, when I came back to his house among the rocks, Eichkao was out of

Epatka, the sea-parrot.

sight, and there lay out on the bank a bill made of red sealing wax, a white mask, and two little white quill pens. There were a few bones and claws and some feathers, but they did not seem to belong to anything in particular, and the little foxes in the rocks went gurgle, gurgle, gurgle.

One day I lay down on the moss out by the old fox walk on the Mist Island, and Eichkao saw me there, and thought I was some new kind of walrus, which might be good to eat and would feed all the little foxes for a month. So he ran around me in a circle, and then he ran round again, then again and again, always making the circle smaller, till finally the circle was so small that I could reach him with my hand. As he went around and around, all the time he looked at me with his cold, gray, selfish eye, and not one of all the beasts has an eye so cruel-cold as his. When he thought that he was near enough he gave a snap with his jaws and tried to bite out a morsel to take home to the little foxes, but all I offered him was a piece of rubber boot. And when I turned around to look at him he was running away as fast as he could, calling clin-n-g-g, clin-n-g, clin-n-g like a scared buzz saw all the time as he went out of sight. And I think that he is running yet, and the little foxes still go gurgle, gurgle, gurgle, under the rocks.

HE was just a bird when he was born, and a very ugly bird at that. For he had big splay-feet with all the toes turned forward and joined together in one broad web, and his wings were thick and

Señor Alcatraz.

clumsy, and underneath his long bill there was a big red sac that he could fill with fishes, and when it

242

was full he could hardly walk or fly, so large was
the sac and so great was his appetite.

But he kept the sac well filled, and he emptied
it out every day into his stomach, and so he grew
very soon to be a large bird, as big as a turkey,
though not as fat, and each day uglier than ever.

But one morning when he was walking out on
the sand flat of the Astillero at Mazatlan, Mexico,
where he lived, he saw a big fish which had been left
by the falling tide in a little pool of water. It was
a blue-colored fish with a big, bony head, and no
scales, and a sleek, slippery skin. He did not know
that it was a Bagre, but thought that all fishes were
good to eat, so he opened his mouth and slipped
the fish, tail first, down into his pouch. It went all
right for a while, but when the fish woke up and
knew he was being swallowed, he straightened out
both of his arms, and there he was. For the Bagre
is a kind of catfish, and each arm is a long, stiff,
sharp bone, or spine, with a saw edge the whole
length of it. And all the Bagre has to do is just to
put this arm out straight and twist it at the shoulder
and then it is set, and no animal can bend or break
it. And it pierced right through the skin of the
bird's sac, and the bird could not swallow it, nor

make it go up nor down, and the Bagre held on tight
for he knew that if he let go once he would be swallowed, and that would be the last of him.

So the bird tried everything he could think of,
and the fish held on, and they kept it up all day. In
the afternoon a little boy came out on the sands.
His name was Inocente, and he was the son of
Ygnacio, the fisherman of Mazatlan. And Inocente
took a club of mangrove and ran up to the struggling
bird, and struck it on the wing with the club. The
blow broke the wing and the bird lay down to die,
for with a broken wing and a fish that would not
go up nor down, there was no hope for him.

When Inocente saw what kind of a fish it was,
he knew just what to do. He reached down into
the bird's sac, and took hold of the fish's spine.
He gave each bone a twist so that it rolled over in its
socket, the upper part toward the fish's head, and
then they were not stiff any more, but lay flat against
the side of the fish, just as they ought to lie. Then
the fish knew that it had found a master and lay
perfectly still. So the bird gave a great gulp and
out the Bagre went on the sand, and when the tide
came up it swam away, and took care never to go
again where a bird could get hold of it. And the

bird with the broken wing had learned something about fishes too. But it could not fly away, so it waited to see what the boy was going to do.

The boy took the bird into his boat and brought him home. And old Ygnacio put a splint on his wing and covered it with salve, and by and by it healed. But the bone was set crooked and the bird could not fly, so the boys called the bird Señor Alcatraz, which is the Spanish for Mr. Pelican, and Señor Alcatraz and all the boys and dogs and goats became good friends, and all ran about on the streets together. And when the boys would shout and the dogs bark, all Señor Alcatraz could do was to squawk and hiss and open his big mouth wide and show the inside of his red fish-sac.

And when the boys would go fishing on the wharf Alcatraz would go too, and he would stow away the fishes in his pouch just as fast as the boys would catch them. But if they caught a Bagre-fish, he would turn his head the other way and then run away home just as fast as he could.

And when the men drew the net on the beach, Alcatraz would splash around inside the net, catching whatever he could, and having lots of fun in his clumsy pelican fashion. Then he would run along the street with the boys, squawking and flapping his wings and thinking that he was just like them. And if you ever go to Mazatlan, ask for Dr. George Warren Rogers, and he will show you the way to Ygnacio's cabin on the street they call Libertad. And there in the front yard, in a general scramble of dogs, goats, and little Indian boys, you will see Señor Alcatraz romping and squabbling like the best of them. And you will know which he is by the broken wing and the red sac under his throat. But if you say Bagre to him, he will run under the doorstep, and hide his face till you go away.

HOW THE COMMANDER SAILED.

(With acknowledgments to Peter Lauridsen.)

"Through fog to fog, by luck and log,
Sail ye as Bering sailed."—*Kipling.*

ONCE there was a great sea captain. He was born in Jutland in 1681, and his name was Vitus Bering. But when he went away from Denmark and became a commander in the Russian navy they called him Ivan Ivanovich Bering, for that was easier for the Russians to say. Captain Bering was a man of great stature, and greater heart, strong, brave, and patient, and so the Russians chose him to lead the gigantic work of the exploration of Siberia and North America.

Thus it chanced that in the spring of 1741 Vitus Bering found himself in the little village of Petropaulski—the harbor of Peter and Paul—which is the capital of the vast uninhabitable region of moss, volcanoes, mosquitoes, and mountain torrents, they call Kamtchatka.

17

And from the village of Peter and Paul Bering sailed forth on his little ship, which he called the "Su Petr," to explore the Icy Sea and to find North America and to learn how to reach it from Kamtchatka. There were seventy-seven men all told on board the Su Petr, or St. Peter, and one of them was George Wilhelm Steller, clear-headed, warm-hearted, and imperious, the naturalist from Halle, born at Winsheim in Franconia in 1709, who has told the story of the voyage.

First they sailed for Gamaland, a great island which on the Russian maps of that day lay in the ocean to the southeast of Kamtchatka. But when the St. Peter came to where Gamaland was, they saw "only sea and sky," a few wandering birds, and no land at all. There never was any Gamaland; but Bering did not know this, so he was surprised to find no land nearer than the bottom of the sea.

The east wind blew and the great fogs hid the sun and stars, but still Bering sailed on. Away over the sea where Gamaland was not, away to the eastward, on and on, till at last they saw before them a great belt of land. The coast was high and jagged, covered with snow in July, lined with green, moss-grown islands, between which the sea swept in swift currents. Over the scrubby forests of stunted fir a snow-capped mountain towered so high that they could see it seventy miles away. "I do not remember," Steller wrote, "of having seen a higher mountain in all Siberia and Kamtchatka." And he was right, for there is none other so high in all the Russian dominions. As it was the day of St. Elias, they named the mountain for the saint, and the bay and the cape and the island—everything they saw—was named for St. Elias. And they are named for St. Elias to this day, all but the island which is called Kayak. They found no inhabitants in St. Elias-land. The people had all run away in fear at the sight of the ship and the white men. But they found a house of timber with a fireplace, a bark basket, a wooden spade, some mussel-shells, and a whetstone, used to sharpen copper knives. Besides these articles they found in an earth hut "some smoked fish, a broken arrow, and the remains of a fire." Some of these things they took away with them. So to make everything fair, Bering left in the house "an iron kettle, a pound of tobacco, a Chinese pipe, and a piece of silk cloth." But no one was there when the people returned to see what use they made of these unexpected presents.

They did not stay long about the Bay of St. Elias. Bering knew that the short summer was far spent, and that if they were to learn anything of the coast they must sail rapidly. · With their few provisions and their small ship they could not spend the winter in this rough country. Many men have blamed him for going away so soon. Whether Bering did right it is not for us to say. We know Steller's opinion, but Bering's we have not heard. Steller said : "The only reason for leaving was stupid obstinacy, fear of a handful of natives, and pusillanimous homesickness. For ten years Bering had equipped himself for this great enterprise; the exploration lasted ten hours." "We have gone over to the New World," he said, " simply to bring American water to Asia."

But however this may be, Bering had none too much time for his return to Kamtchatka. Half his crew was sick already, and the rest were none too strong. Those who would stay here longer, Bering said, forget "how far we are from home and what may yet befall us." So the St. Peter sailed homeward on the wings of a southeast gale. In the mist and fog the coast was invisible, though the soundings showed that land was not far away. Islands they sighted from time to time, inhospitable headlands, green at the top and black on the sides, where the great surf broke before the constant gales. They sighted the high point of Marmot Island; then sailed around the great island of Kadiak. They narrowly escaped shipwreck on an island called The Foggy One—but every island is foggy in those wild storm-washed seas.

From time to time they saw the tall, snow-capped volcanoes of the mainland—Pavlof and Shishaldin and Progromnia, and all the rest of them. They passed close behind the seven high rocks we call to-day the Semidi. And whenever the sun shone for a day the sea grew rougher than ever, for in the Icy Seas a break in the clouds is the signal for a new storm.

Salted meats and hard biscuit without change of diet brought on the disease called scurvy. This comes when men eat too much salt without fruit or vegetables, and it shows itself in loosened teeth, which fall out of the shrunken gums. Affairs grew worse and worse. Bering and more than half of his men were sick, and when they came to thirteen rag-ged, barren islands which rise above the surf in the thick mist, they landed there and carried the sick

ones ashore. One of the sailors named Shumágin
died here, and so the islands are called Shumágin to
this day.

While the men searched for fresh water on these
islands, Steller looked everywhere for roots and berries with which to heal the men sick with scurvy.
The "molino" berry, the most delicious in all the
world, grows on these islands. It is a sort of raspberry, very large, amber-colored, juicy, and with a
rich wild flavor that no raspberry of the South can
yield. Bering was wonderfully helped by the berries,
and might have recovered had they been able to stay
on shore long enough to drive away the scurvy. The
medicine chest of the ship, it was said, contained
"plasters and salves for half an army," but no reme-
dies for men who were hurt inwardly by the poor
salt food.

At the Shumágin Islands the sailors filled their
water casks, but they took water from a pond into
which the surf had broken, and when they came to
drink it the salt made the scurvy worse than ever.
One of their boats was wrecked as they went on, and
they had trouble with the Aleut people on the shores.
Still they sailed on, with the east wind behind and
the thick cloud-rack overhead.

Then the wind blew from the west instead, and from time to time it rose to a hurricane. "I know of no harder, more fatiguing life," wrote one of Bering's officers, "than to sail an unknown sea." And of all the seas in the world none is rougher than the one the St. Peter sailed, and none has such a wilderness of inhospitable islands to mark its boundaries. When Bering's men thought they were halfway home they saw land to the north of them, still another wild, inhospitable cliff, topped by a snowy volcano. They called the island St. Johannes, but its real name is Atka, and there are many more such before one comes to the end of the island chain, where the far west joins "the unmitigated east." Still they sailed against the west wind, which Steller said "seemed to issue from a flue, with such a whistling, roaring, and rumbling that we expected every moment to lose mast and rudder or to see the ship crushed between the breakers. The dashing of the heavy sea against the vessel sounded like cannon." The sailors could not stand erect on the ship. They could not cook. The few who were well remained so because they did not dare to get sick. All lost "their firmness of purpose; their courage became unsteady as their teeth." Still they sailed on. It was as easy to do that as to return. Still another snow-topped island, Amchitka, came in view to the north, again to their great surprise, for they thought they were in the open sea. They knew nothing of the long line of Aleutian volcanoes which pass in a great bow from Alaska across to Kamtchatka. They sailed past Attu, the last of the Aleutian Islands. After a time they came to a long steep coast running north and south, which they took for Kamtchatka. Every one was overjoyed. Bering crawled from his bed to the deck, revived by the sight of what seemed to be friendly land, and in such fashion as they could and with such beverages as were left, they celebrated their "happy return."

But though the land they found was very differ- ent from the Aleutian Islands, and bore no volcano at its summit, they could not recognize it, nor did they find it hospitable. Medni Island is a narrow backbone of rock, shaped like a cross-cut saw, with wild, hollowed-out, storm-beaten cliffs and great reefs, over which the surf breaks from the deep green waves. There were no inhabitants, no harbors, no landing places, and the winds came down in wild gusts, or "willie waughs" from the snow-covered craggy heights. A storm carried away their mainsail. As they drifted along to the northward the land came to an end in a cluster of jagged rocks. So this could not be Kamtchatka. Their joy gave way to direst distress.

The sailors broke out in mutiny. Nobody cared for the ship. It drifted on to the west with the gentle wind beating against a little sail at its foremast, but the St. Peter had no longer either helmsman or commander.

Soon another island loomed up before them, a shore of great flat-topped mountains, ending in huge, black, vertical cliffs at the sea. In a clear night they came to anchor in a little bay to the north of a black promontory, now called Tolstoi Mys—the thick cape. In the great surf "the ship was tossed like a ball," the cable of their anchor snapped, and the vessel came near being crushed on the jagged rocks of the shore.

In the morning they landed in the little sandy bay north of Tolstoi, and set out to search for inhabitants. They found none, for Bering's men were the first who ever set foot on the twin Storm Islands. The little bay was surrounded by high, craggy steeps, without trees, overgrown by dense moss, and cut by swift brooks. The sailors, under Steller's direction,

built a house in the sand, and covered it with a roof
of driftwood and turf, and made its walls of the
frozen carcasses of the foxes they had killed for their
skins.   Everywhere swarmed the little kit-foxes, blue
foxes, and white foxes, Eichkao and all his hungry
family.   Those of the sailors who died were devoured
by them almost before they could be buried.   Other
little huts they made of driftwood and foxes, their
floors dug out of the sand.   And the foxes who were
alive snapped and snarled about the houses made of
the foxes who were dead.   And all winter long the
men sought far and wide on the rocky coast for driftwood, and dug it out of the ten feet of snow under
which it was buried.

The Commander Bering, still helpless, was placed
in one of these huts.   The vessel when he had left it
was beached by a storm, and the crew dragged it up
into the sand where it lay all winter.   The little
blue fox, the most greedy and selfish of beasts, hung
around the camp the winter long, attacking the sick
and devouring the dead, almost before the eyes of
their friends.   Of the seventy-seven, thirty-one died,
among them Bering himself.   "He was," Steller said,
" buried alive; the sand kept constantly rolling down
upon him from the sides of the pit and covered

his feet. At first this was removed, but finally he asked that it might remain, as it furnished him a little of the warmth he so sorely needed. Soon half his body was under the sand and his comrades had to dig him out to give him a decent burial."

So perished the great Commander at the age of sixty years. The island where he died has ever since then been called Bering Island. The twin "Storm Islands," Bering and Medni (Copper) Islands, have been called for him Komandorski, the Islands of the Commander, and the great Icy Sea is known as Bering Sea. And his life and work, says Lauridsen, will ever stand as "a living testimony of what northern perseverance is able to accomplish even with the most humble means."

In the spring of 1742, Steller and the rest made of the wreck of the St. Peter an open boat, in which they traversed the one hundred and fifty miles of the Icy Sea between Bering Island and Petropaulski, and if we should follow them further we should only bring them into deeper trouble. Their friends at Petropaulski had divided and spent all the property they had left. When they went back in poverty to Russia, some rival accused Steller of having sold powder to enemies of the Czar. Sent back to

Siberia for trial, he had to ride in an open sleigh drawn by dogs. His guards went one night into a wayside inn, leaving him outside in the sleigh to fall asleep with weariness. When they came out warmed and filled, Steller was frozen to death. Thus died in his thirty-fifth year one of the most devoted of naturalists and bravest of men, and his work was made known through the hands of others.

For a long time, at Bering Island, Steller and his men did not dare to touch the bones of the Russian ship, for the Czar who owned the St. Peter is swift to punish any injury to his property. But they feared the knout less than they feared death by storm and starvation. So in the name of the Czar, Steller condemned the St. Peter as no longer seaworthy, released her from the Russian service, and then his men made a little boat out of the wreck that remained.

Their stay on Bering Island is forever famous for the discovery of the "four great beasts" of the sea, on the account of which Steller's fame as a naturalist rests. These were the Sea Cow, the Sea Otter, the Sea Lion, and the Sea Bear.

In the giant kelp which grows on all the sunken reefs, like the tawny mane of some huge animal, the sea cow had her home. A huge, blundering, harmless beast, feeding on kelp, shaped like a whale in body, but with a cow-like head, a split upper lip, and a homely, amiable appearance, as befits a beast who looks like an ogre and feeds like a cow. The creature was forty feet in length, and weighed about three tons. Bering's men soon found that the sea cow made good sea-steaks. They lived on her meat, and the sailors who came after them in years to come devoured and destroyed them all. The last sea cow was killed in 1768, and its bones are now among the treasures of the great museums, the greatest number of them being in the National Museum at Washington.

Next came the sea otter, a creature as large as a big dog, with long gray fur, the finest of all fur for cloaks and overcoats. The sea otter lived in the sea about the islands, the female swimming around in the kelp, with her young in her arms, and making long trips from place to place in search of food. A shy, timid, suspicious creature, the sea otter is hard to kill and easy to drive away; and of the countless millions which existed in Steller's time only a few hundred remain.

The great gray sea lion was a ponderous beast like the fur seal in figure and habits, but much larger, the male weighing almost a ton. His huge head is

like that of a St. Bernard dog, and his roar is one of
the grandest sounds on earth. It is a rich, mellow
double bass, like the voice of a mighty organ, and it
can be heard for miles. The female is much smaller,
also yellowish gray in color, and she too has a rich
bass voice, an octave higher than that of the male.
When a herd of sea lions are driven into the sea, they
will rise out of the surf at once and all together, roaring in melody. Such a wonderful chorus can be
heard nowhere else on earth, and it is no wonder
that the lion of the sea made a great impression on
Steller. The sea lions live in families on the rocks,
where the males fight for supremacy, often over-
turning huge boulders in their struggles. The young
are cinnamon-colored, and when they are born they
look much like female fur seals, and are almost as
large. And when the old males are fighting they
toddle away, and if they do not they are crushed
under the rocks that are rolled about, or else tram-
pled on by huge, flappy feet.

Most interesting of all the great beasts of the sea
was the one Steller called the sea bear—or, as men
now call it, the " fur seal."

These creatures came on shore by the thousands
on the west coast of Bering Island when the ice left

the shores in the spring. They made their homes on the rocks of Poludionnoye, a great city of beasts each year rising from the sea.

But the story of how the beachmasters and their families behave on Bering and Medni and St. Paul and St. George and Robben, has been many times told and in many ways, so I need not give it here.

But we can imagine how Steller looked down on the slopes of Poludionnoye, and saw the old beachmasters roar and groan and weep and blow out their musky breath, as they fought for supremacy. We can see with him the trim ranks of sleek and dainty Matkas tripping up the beach as they come back from the long swim. We can imagine the great groups of snug Kotiks that clustered about the warring beachmasters, while along the shores up and down wandered and played the hosts of young bachelors eager to keep near the homes, but afraid to enter them till their wigs and tusks were grown. We can see them in countless hosts, trooping, playing, sleeping on the sands, reckless of drives, and unharmed by clubs, and we can understand the splendid enthusiasm with which the discoverer of all these things wrote of the four great "Beasts of the Sea."

And as for Bering, the Commander, as a recompense for all pain and disappointment and loss stands the fact that he was the first. His for all time are the twin Storm Islands, where the St. Peter was wrecked, and Bering's forever shall be the Icy Sea. And all who go there shall do homage to the name and fame of the great Commander, and all who love the huge beasts of the sea will remember the naturalist who first saw them and who first told their story.

Medni Island, as seen from Tolstoi Mys where Bering died.

CAPE CHEERFUL.

"When you shall come to a great cliff standing northward from Ma-kushin, the Volcano, and rent almost from base to summit and from the midst of which leaps the tumultuous Waterfall sheer into the Sea, then, the fog lifting, you will leave the cliff well to Starboard, and enter a land-locked haven called Captain's Harbor, for that I did once ride out the winter there. Whence is this Headland with the Waterfall called 'Cape Cheerful.'"—*Log book attributable to Captain Cook, Unalaska, 1778.*

HOMEWARD bound from the Storm Islands
  through the sullen Icy Sea;
    On our lee
Rise the savage, swart Smoke Islands which defy
    Sea and sky,
Hurling back the waves insistent from their boulder-
  cumbered shore,
    Evermore.
All at once the drifting cloud-rack seems to fall
    Like a wall,
And the twin Smoke Islands vanish as a specter of
  the night
    From our sight,
While the ship still plunges onward, fog-bound in
  the Icy Sea.
    Suddenly,

18   263

As the light is slowly failing—the long twilight of
    the North—
             Rises forth,
As though shattering the cloud-rack grim and tall,
             The lava-wall
Of the shapeless huge Moss Island with her earth-
    quake-riven cliff;
             Through the rift,
Like a swift-spun skein of silver, springs intact
             The cataract
From the black basaltic buttress prone into the Icy
    Sea;
             Joyfully
Does it join the tumbling billows, while its spray
             Drifts away
With the east wind to the leeward. Banished now
    is every fear,
             All is clear,
For we know the cape called Cheerful, and it tells
    the haven near.

.   .   .   .

Sometimes like the surly ocean seems the weary
    course of life:
             Doubt and strife
Hide the way I fain would follow: can I know
             What to do?

Slowly down my path I wander, sore-perplexed,
                    Spirit-vexed,
By the cloud-rack of conventions o'er us all,
                    Like a pall;
Thus with downcast eyes and sombre come I to the
    garden gate.
                    Swift and straight,
Leaping from a bank of roses, like a fetterless cas-
    cade,
                    Unafraid
Rush the children forth to greet me with a joyous
    shout of cheer.
Banished now is all convention, all vexation, and con-
    tention,
                    All is clear:
I have found the cape called "Cheerful,"
        And I know the haven near.

H. M. S. Pheasant,
    Off Cape Cheerful, Unalaska,
        September 1, 1896.

THE END.

www.ingramcontent.com/pod-product-compliance
Lightning Source LLC
Chambersburg PA
CBHW020339030726
47496CB00007B/1947